Rae snatched her fingers away from the sheet of paper as if it were on fire. But the thoughts kept coming.

YOU NEED TO BE BACK IN THIS HOSPITAL. SAFE IN YOUR OWN LITTLE ROOM. STRAPPED IN YOUR OWN LITTLE BED.

Those thoughts aren't coming from fingerprints, Rae thought. *And they aren't coming from me. They aren't.*

But wasn't that what all lunatics thought? That the voices in their heads were from God or dogs or aliens or something?

Have I been crazy all this time? Am I going to end up in here for the rest of my life? Rae was sure those thoughts were her own. And they froze the blood in her veins.

Don't miss any of the books in this
thrilling new series:

fingerprints

fingerprints ™

6

revelations

melinda metz

AVON BOOKS
An Imprint of HarperCollins*Publishers*

Revelations

Printed in the United States of America.

For information address
HarperCollins Children's Books, a division of
HarperCollins Publishers, 1350 Avenue of the Americas,
New York, NY 10019.

 Produced by 17th Street Productions,
an Alloy Online, Inc. company
33 West 17th Street, New York, NY 10011

Library of Congress Catalog Card Number: 2001116860
ISBN 0-06-447283-3

First Avon edition, 2001

AVON TRADEMARK REG. U.S. PAT. OFF.
AND IN OTHER COUNTRIES,
MARCA REGISTRADA, HECHO EN U.S.A.

Visit us on the World Wide Web!
www.harperteen.com

For the New York City writers who cheered me on,
inspired me, and cracked the whip as I worked on this
series—Tatiana Akoeva, Beth Butler, Adrienne Foran,
Marilyn Horowitz, Claire Moed, and most especially
Shirley Kwan—with gobs of appreciation and affection.

revelations

Okay, *you can do this,* Rae Voight thought. *You have to do this.* She peered down the hallway she knew Anthony would use to get to the cafeteria. She didn't want to see Anthony. Not now. Not ever. Which was why she'd been avoiding him for days. But she had to talk to him. He had a right to know how things had ended. Until she told him, she couldn't get on with her life. And that's all she wanted. To get on with her normal-girl life with her so-far-above-normal-former-ex-boyfriend Marcus Salkow.

Thinking of Marcus made her feel all cozy, like she'd been wrapped in her favorite fuzzy blanket. *A few minutes with Anthony, then it can be all Marcus all the time,* Rae promised herself. She took another look down the hall. *Come on, Anthony, come on,* she thought. *I want to get this over with.*

An electric tingle ran down Rae's spine. And a moment later she saw Anthony heading toward her. It was like the rest of her body recognized him before her eyes did. Except no. No. There was no reason for a surge of energy to run through her just because Anthony Fascinelli was in the vicinity.

Rae nervously fluffed her curly, reddish brown hair. She wished she'd worn shoes with higher heels. It would feel good to be taller than Anthony during this conversation. Maybe she should wait until tomorrow and—

No, Rae ordered herself. *You are doing this. Right here. Right now.* "Anthony," she called out before she could change her mind. He reached her way too quickly. She wasn't ready. She—

"Steve Mercer is dead," she blurted. "So no one's after me anymore. I just wanted you to know because . . . because in a way he was after you, too, since you were helping me. So thanks. And have a nice life."

Anthony blinked. "Back up," he demanded, staring at her as if she were speaking another language. "*Who* is Steve Mercer?"

Like you care, Rae wanted to scream at him. Instead she pulled in a long, slow breath. Somehow it had all blurred together in her mind . . . what Anthony knew and what he didn't know. Maybe because she was trying her hardest not to know any of it anymore, to just forget it had ever happened.

"Steve Mercer was a scientist," she explained. "He was in charge of that group my mother was in."

"Right. The group," Anthony agreed. He paused. "Hold on—a scientist? I don't get it. What exactly was the group about?"

Rae swallowed. Why couldn't Anthony just let her get through this quickly?

"The group was—they were people who had some kind of special ability," she said. She glanced around the hallway almost out of habit, then reminded herself that no one was after her anymore. "And Mercer's job was to get the people in the group to develop major psi powers," she continued, focusing her gaze back on Anthony. "Drugs, radiation, shock treatment—you name it, Steve did it to them. To my mom," she added in a softer voice.

"And it worked," Anthony said, his brown eyes wide in amazement.

"Yeah, it worked so well that I ended up . . . you know," Rae said. "And that's why Mercer was after me. I guess the guy went kind of nuts. He decided that what he'd done to the members of the group was dangerous to society. So he basically went on a little killing spree. He killed my mom and at least one other person from the group. Maybe more. And he watched the kids who were born after the experiment. Watched us our whole lives. When he saw that I had been affected, he decided he needed to kill me, too."

Rae shook her head hard. "But you don't need to know all this. What you need to know is that it's over. Mercer's dead. Guys from the government agency that funded the experiments killed him. So no one's going to be attempting to massacre me again. No one's going to get kidnapped."

"That's great. That's so freakin' great." Anthony reached for her. Rae jumped away, scraping her back against the corner of the trophy case behind her. How could he even think of touching her after what he'd done to her?

"Freakin' great," Rae repeated. "Yeah. Exactly. So what I wanted to tell you is your life can go back to normal. Yours and Yana's." The name Yana felt like it was made of razor blades. Rae was surprised her mouth didn't start bleeding the second she'd gotten the name out.

"Rae . . . I . . ." Anthony jammed his hands into his pockets. "I should have told you that Yana and I had hooked up. I shouldn't have—"

"What?" Rae interrupted. "Shouldn't have destroyed

my little sweet-sixteen birthday dinner by showing up with Yana?"

"It's not like you and I were ever—" Anthony began to protest.

"I thought we were friends," Rae interrupted. "That's what I thought we were. And then you got together with Yana just so I'd know how it felt to have someone go behind my back. Even though I only looked for your dad because I wanted to help, and I didn't even send Yana's dad that stupid letter."

"The letter about treating Yana better? What does that have to do with—"

"Yes, that letter. Don't bother pretending to be so innocent, Anthony," Rae cut in again. "I know you and Yana got together as payback. She *told* me. She thought I went behind her back with the letter, so she decided to go behind mine. And you went along for the ride."

"You just assume I was in on it, right?" Anthony said, his voice flat. "You don't even ask me. You just assume. Because that's just the kind of thing I'd do."

"So you started going out with my best friend because you—" Rae began.

This time Anthony interrupted her. "Because she's hot, okay? And it's not like you and I were—"

"But you kissed me," Rae accused. "And then you were sticking your tongue down Yana's throat

5

two seconds later." She pressed the heels of her hands against her forehead, then dropped her arms to her sides. "This isn't what I wanted to say to you. I just wanted you to know that everything is over and that you, Jesse, me, we're all safe."

Rae forced herself to meet Anthony's gaze. Usually his eyes reminded her of melted Hershey's Kisses. But right now they were hard and cold. "Thanks. Thanks for what you did for me."

"Yeah, thanks, and now you that you have no use for me, I should just get away from you, right, Rae?"

"It was your choice," she muttered. Then she had to look away. She felt like Anthony's eyes were turning her to ice. "Oh, there's Marcus. I should go." She didn't wait for an answer. She just rushed over to Marcus and hurled herself at him, wrapping her arms around his neck.

"Hi," Marcus mumbled against her lips.

Rae didn't answer. She closed her eyes, wanting to lose herself in the taste of Marcus. Just kiss him and kiss him and kiss him.

"Maybe we should take this to my car," Marcus finally said, pulling away half an inch.

"Maybe," Rae agreed. She slid her arm around his waist, turned him toward the nearest exit—and saw Mr. Jesperson staring at them. The teacher creeped her out, always so interested in how she was *doing,* but Rae forced herself to smile at him, anyway. *Look at me, Mr. Jesperson,* she thought. *I'm fine. I'm more than fine. You don't have to worry about poor, troubled Rae Voight anymore. I have my life back. And I'm going to make it perfect. Perfect with Marcus.*

"I know we're going to the car," Rae told Marcus. "But I think I have to kiss you again right here."

Anthony felt his lips heat up. Like he was the one kissing Rae instead of Marcus. *But you're not,* he told himself. *She's made it glass clear that you're dead as far as she's concerned. Dead and rotting.*

Saliva flooded his mouth, and he got that about-to-puke feeling. He had to get out of there. Anthony turned on his heel and strode back down the hall and out into the parking lot. He pulled in gulps of the crisp fall air until his stomach stopped trying to jerk itself up his throat, then he headed over to his car—technically his mom's car—and got in. He put the Hyundai in reverse and backed out of the parking spot so fast that the motion threw his body back against the seat. He didn't care. He had to get out of there. Away from Rae. Rae and Marcus and kissing. Now, now, now.

Anthony just drove. He didn't care where he was going as long as it was away. At least that's what he thought until he realized he was heading to Yana's school. He did a cop check of the street, then pressed the gas pedal down a little farther. Less than two minutes later he was parked in front of the school. He didn't want to waste time looking for her, so he asked the security guard at the closest entrance where to find the main office. After the guy did a friggin' inspection of Anthony's ID, he pointed Anthony down a hallway to the left. Anthony held himself to a walk, even though he wanted to put down his head and plow the way he did on the football field.

"I'm Yana Savari's cousin," he announced as soon as he was through the office door. "There's a family emergency. I'm supposed to get Yana and take her to the hospital."

Anthony expected to get a bunch of questions, but the girl behind the desk, who didn't look any older than he was, didn't seem to care. She just turned to the computer, hit a few keys, then said, "Room 104. You want to go down there and get her yourself?"

"Yeah. Thanks," Anthony answered, already halfway out the door.

"You take a right, then another right," the girl called after him. Anthony allowed himself to trot down the hall, not run, since running could get him stopped by a random teacher wandering the halls. His sneakers squeaked as he made the second right. He swung his head back and forth as he started down the hall. Room 104. Yeah. Anthony veered over to it, gave a light little knock, then opened the door and leaned inside.

He blurted his cover story to the teacher. She looked dubious, but when he said he'd already been to the office, she let Yana go. Anthony focused his gaze a little to Yana's left as she crossed the room toward him. He couldn't really look at her. If he did, he wasn't sure he'd be able to stop himself from ripping her lying head right off her neck.

Anthony pressed himself against the door frame as Yana walked past him, but her body still brushed against his. The contact got his stomach heaving again. He gave a couple of hard swallows, then, when he was sure he wasn't going to spew right there, he stepped out into the hall after Yana and closed the door behind him.

"You must be psychic or something," Yana told him. "I need to talk to you so badly. My father is—"

"Shut up," Anthony ordered. "I don't want to hear anything out of you. The only reason I'm here is to tell you that I don't want you within one hundred feet of me, ever."

"I'm trying to tell you that—" Yana protested.

"Yeah. I want to hear more of your lies," Anthony cut her off.

Yana's blue eyes became electric, all the vulnerability from a second ago gone. Anthony could almost feel them crackling. "More lies? Exactly what lies have I supposedly told you?"

"Um. Hmmm. What was it?" Anthony snapped. "Oh, yeah. You were using me to get back at Rae for that letter she supposedly sent to your dad. And that makes pretty much everything you've said to me since we started hooking up a lie."

"Oh, and it was so awful for you, wasn't it?" Yana shot back. "Making out with me for hours at a time."

"I'm done with you," Anthony told her. There was no point in having some long, drawn-out conversation about it all. He turned away from Yana and started down the hall away from her. A second later she grabbed his elbow, her grip a lot stronger than he'd expected it to be. She yanked him around to face her.

"Listen, jerk, I had fun with you, okay?" Yana said, not letting go of his arm. "It wasn't just about giving Rae a lesson in how it feels to be backstabbed. I mean, yeah, that was why I started up the thing with you. But I . . . I liked it, you know? And you seemed to be having a pretty good time yourself."

Anthony ripped his arm out of Yana's grip.

"Yeah, I had a good time. Because I was a freakin' moron. I didn't even think about the possibility that—" Anthony shook his head. "This is a waste. I've already said what I came for—to tell you to stay far away from me." He turned and started down the hall again. Nothing she could say, nothing she could do, was going to change his mind. He never wanted to see her lying face again.

Rae ran the tiny brush over the nail of her index finger, enjoying the faint coolness of the polish. And the beauty of its wet mauveness. She smiled, shaking her head. She couldn't believe that she was actually marveling over fingernail polish, like it was so wonderful, it was proof of God's existence.

She couldn't help it, though. Everything felt . . . more precious now, now that her life was her own again. The sensation of her freshly shaved legs brushing against the inside of her khakis was delicious. The splotches of sunlight on her bedroom floor made her want to curl up inside one of them. The sound of her Radiohead CD was vibrating in her bones, and it felt like the music was coming out of her instead of something she was just passively listening to.

I have to hold on to this, Rae thought. *I don't want to ever forget how amazing it is just to be alive.* She began to paint the next naked fingernail. Then the phone rang.

It's Anthony, she thought. *You don't know that,* she corrected herself. *It could be Marcus. It's much more likely that it's Marcus. Marcus is your boyfriend. Marcus is the one taking you to the dance tonight.* Rae gingerly picked up the phone, careful not to do any damage to her wet nails. "Hello."

"Hi, Rae. This is Ms. Abramson."

Oh, goody, my therapist, Rae thought. But a call from Ms. Abramson wasn't enough to shake her out of her glorious mood. Not nearly enough.

"I know we have an individual appointment after the next group session," Ms. Abramson continued, "but I was wondering if we could push it back a few days."

"Yeah, that works for me," Rae answered. "Except I don't know if I really need an individual session. I don't think I need therapy at all anymore. Everything is going so great. I even got back with my old boyfriend. I'm feeling incredible."

"I'm glad to hear it," Ms. Abramson answered. "But ending therapy is a big decision, and it's not something that should be done abruptly. Look, why don't we do an individual appointment after the last group session of this week? We can talk about a strategy for tapering off therapy if we both decide that's what's best for you. How does that sound?"

"Fine," Rae answered. What else could she say? She should have known Ms. Abramson wouldn't just be like, "Wonderful, Rae. You never have to come to therapy again. Have a fabulous life."

"All right. See you in group," Ms. Abramson said.

"Okay. Bye." Rae gently hung up the phone. The mauve of her nail polish didn't seem quite so amazing anymore. *Think about the dance,* Rae ordered herself. *Think about you and Anthony there. Marcus!* she corrected herself. *You and Marcus. Dancing. Him holding you close.*

God, it was probably the dream of more than half the girls in school. And it was Rae's life. She couldn't believe Anthony's name had popped into her head like that. *It's just because you had to deal with him today,* she told herself. *But you did it. You told him what you needed to tell him, and you don't ever have to talk to him again.*

The doorbell rang, pulling Rae out of her thoughts. "It's Anthony," she murmured. She could almost see him out on the porch, wanting a chance to explain to her again that he didn't know what Yana had planned. *But it doesn't matter whether he knew or not,* Rae told herself. *He still went sneaking around with her. He could have told me, but—*

The doorbell rang again. Rae stood up, glad she hadn't started painting her toenails yet, and hurried to the door. She pulled it open. Her first instinct was to slam it shut. Because Yana was standing there.

As if Yana expected Rae to do just that, she reached out and held the door open with one hand. "I know you hate me right now," she said, and her voice came out all trembly.

"Yeah, I do," Rae told her. She gave the door a shove, but Yana's hand held it open.

"I know. I know. But I need your help, Rae. I really need your help," Yana blurted.

She's been crying, Rae realized, taking in Yana's bloodshot eyes and puffy face. Rae had never seen Yana even close to this upset. *But that's not my problem.* "We're not friends," Rae said. "You can't trust me, remember? You're so sure I went behind your back and sent your dad that letter. I'm the last person you should be coming to. Why don't you go find one of your real friends?"

"You are my friend. My only real friend," Yana said, her voice getting higher with each word.

God, she's about to snap, Rae realized.

"I wouldn't have come here if I wasn't desperate," Yana continued. "I know you don't want to see me. But you're the only one who can help me, Rae. The only one. I need you to use your power."

* * *

I can't stand to think about Rae right now. She's so happy. So sure the world is a wonderful place created just for her. So excited about having her perfect boyfriend back.

14

It makes me sick. Rae doesn't deserve a happy life. She doesn't deserve a life at all. And I'm going to make sure she doesn't have one for long. But before I kill her, I think Rae should be forced to remember that the world isn't her own private toy. I don't want her to die when she's this happy. That's not the revenge that I deserve. I want her to feel all the pain I've been forced to feel. When she has, then it will be time for her to die.

Chapter 2

Anthony pulled off his football helmet, sweat gluing his hair to his head and stinging his eyes. Then he spotted Marcus heading his way. Marcus was the last guy Anthony wanted to see right now. He was just too freakin' happy. When Anthony looked at him, he could practically see Marcus's skin glowing in all the places that Rae had touched him.

Anthony pretended he didn't see Marcus, then leaned over and propped his hands on his knees, trying to look like he was too winded to talk. But Marcus kept on coming, like some overgrown puppy who was sure everyone in the whole wide world wanted to play with him. He stopped next to Anthony and thrust a water bottle into his hand.

"You okay?" Marcus asked. "You took some direct hits today."

"Yeah. Fine," Anthony answered. He took a long swig from the water bottle and handed it back to Marcus. Marcus kept on standing there. Great.

"So, you going to the dance tonight?" Marcus asked. Before Anthony could grunt out a response, Marcus rushed on. "'Cause if you are, you know, could you vote for me and Rae for Moonbeam King and Queen?" Marcus finished off the water and wiped his mouth on his sleeve. "It's not like I care," he added quickly. "I mean, being the stupid Moonbeam King isn't a big deal or anything. But I know Rae'd be into winning."

Rae. Of course Marcus had to bring up Rae. Her name was like a hot poker digging into Anthony's brain, somehow activating an explosion of memories. Rae floating in the water of the Y pool, her body lightly resting in his hands. Rae walking into the middle of a robbery Anthony and some guys were about to pull to stop Anthony from doing something stupid. Rae working a piece of clay into a hand. Rae unconscious on the floor of the Motel 6. Rae looking at him like he'd hurt her more than she even knew she was able to be hurt.

"Not my kind of deal," Anthony muttered, the last image of Rae locked into his head. *This is what hell is,* he thought. *Being forced to look at her face forever. See the pain. Know I caused it.*

"There'd be girls all over you," Marcus said. "That freshman pom-pom, the one with the hair, she practically drools when she looks at you."

Anthony pulled the top of his football jersey over his face and scrubbed it hard. The image of Rae didn't fade. "Oh, yeah, drool. That's sexy," he answered, trying to sound like he wasn't in the middle of being frickin' tortured.

"It's not just her—" Marcus began.

"Gotta hit the showers," Anthony cut him off. Maybe holding his head under the spray for a couple of hours would wash away the picture of Rae. If it didn't, he'd just have to get a knife and hack it out, carve right through his skull and whack, whack, whack.

He trotted toward the gym, then came to a stop as he caught sight of the parking lot out of the corner of his eye. Rae's birthday present was still in the Hyundai. It was a stupid little thing—one of those little "world's best teacher" statues, like something a first grader would give his teacher at the end of the year. But Rae might think it was cute.

Rae's hurt face flashed through his head. *Yeah, moron,* he told himself. *A cheap, stupid present is going to make Rae feel all better.*

Anthony veered toward his car, anyway. Rae's

teaching him to read was probably the best thing anybody had ever done for him. She deserved the teacher statue. Even if all she did was snap the thing's head off while screaming what a jerk Anthony was, she should have it.

He popped open the lock of the passenger side door, opened it, and pulled the little package out of the glove compartment. The sheet of the Sunday comic section he'd used as wrapping paper was looking a little grungy, but whatever. He wanted to get the present into Rae's locker today so it would be there for her when she got to school in the morning.

Anthony slammed the car door shut and headed for the main entrance. *Will Rae be pissed when she realizes I went into her locker without asking?* he worried as he pushed though the double doors. *Yeah, Anthony,* he answered himself as he made his way down the hall. *She's going to really hate you for using the locker combo she gave you. That's a lot worse than hooking up with her supposed best friend without even saying one word to her.*

Rae's agonized face continued to push its way into his mind. Anthony picked up the pace until he was running full out. *It'll go away once I put the present in the locker,* he thought, although he didn't believe himself.

He turned the corner into the hallway where

Rae's locker was and skidded to a stop. "I don't frickin' believe this," he whispered, feeling his muscles clench. Who could have done this? Who could have done this to Rae?

Not important now, he told himself, trying to control the anger rising up in him. He turned around and strode to the guys' bathroom. He rolled the handle on the towel dispenser until the strip of rough brown paper towel was long enough to touch the floor. Then he ripped it off, got it wet, and covered it with gritty pink soap powder. Rae was not going to see what Anthony had just seen.

Anthony hurried out of the bathroom and back over to Rae's locker. He paused for a second, staring at the mess, his body going to steel again. He could barely believe what he was looking at.

The word *unclean* was scrawled across Rae's locker in dripping red letters. Anthony balled up the sopping paper towel and scrubbed until the muscles in his arm were screaming. The word was still faintly visible. *Unclean.* Anthony went back to the bathroom for more paper towels and soap.

"Why don't you go tell Anthony your problems?" Rae demanded. She gave the front door a hard shove. Yana grunted, but she kept her arm straight so that the door couldn't close.

"Anthony hates me even more than you do, if that's possible," Yana answered.

Don't believe her, Rae told herself. *You know you can't believe anything she says. She's a liar. Remember that.*

"He wasn't in on the . . . you know, on trying to get back at you for the letter," Yana added. "He just—"

"Hooked up with you and then went sneaking around. Almost like he knew he had something to be ashamed of," Rae interrupted, although she was unable to keep a few glowing specks of relief from appearing inside her. Anthony at least hadn't tried to maul her heart. He was just an idiot.

Yana opened her mouth, but Rae cut her off before she could speak another word. "Look, I don't care who you go to with your *issue.* I'm not—"

"Weren't you listening?" Yana burst out. "You're the only one who can help me, Rae. No one else. Just you. Without your power—" Yana stopped and shook her head. "This isn't what I meant to say. I'm going to start over."

A long beat of silence stretched out between them. Finally Rae forced herself to meet Yana's gaze. It seemed to be the signal Yana was waiting for. "I'm sorry," Yana said. "That was the first thing I was going to say. Even though it's so pathetic. Like saying two words changes anything." Yana grimaced.

"I'm sorry," she muttered. Her eyes skittered away from Rae's for a moment, then Yana locked gazes with Rae again.

Rae waited. Yana obviously wasn't going to leave until she spat out her little speech. But that didn't mean Rae had to help her out.

"My dad, he went ballistic when he got that letter," Yana said. "I still don't get why he gave a crap that somebody thought he wasn't being the kind of dad he should be. Like did he actually think he was a father-of-the-year contender or something?" Yana shrugged. "Whatever, for some reason, he went off. He started screaming about how I was screwing up his life. How people were sniffing around him because of me. It didn't help that a week before the letter arrived, the principal of my school made him have a meeting with her. He was none too pleased about that, either. Although again, I don't know why he gave a crap." Yana stopped short. "I'm doing it again. This isn't what I was going to talk about. I know you don't care about this garbage."

Rae let her keep talking, waiting her out. She shifted her weight from one foot to the other, unable to help noticing that Yana was definitely pretty upset about something—it took a lot for her to lose her cool like this. In fact, the only other time Rae had seen her so freaked was when they'd been kidnapped together.

"Like I said," Yana finally went on, "I'm sorry that I blamed you for the letter. When it first came, I just kind of went nuts. I was sure you'd sent it. It was the only thing that made sense to me." Yana sucked in a long breath. "Then later—after I went to your school and spewed all over you—I started to think I might be wrong. You never gave me any reason to do something like that. And the more I thought about what you said to me that day at your school . . . well, we did both think someone was listening to our conversations in the Motel 6."

"If you started thinking all that, then—" Rae began.

"Just let me get all this out, okay?" Yana interrupted. "I really knew you didn't do it—at least after I managed to grow a brain again. But I don't know, I'd made such a huge thing of it. I'd already totally screwed our friendship. And so I guess I pretended to myself that I didn't know what I knew, if that makes any sense."

Rae pressed her lips together. "I know what you mean," she admitted. She'd definitely had quite a few times in the last months where she didn't want to accept the reality that was being shoved in her face. "But it's still no excuse for what you did to me, Yana."

"This is no excuse, either," Yana told her. "But I'm going to say it, anyway. It's just that while my dad was doing his lunatic act and I was still trying to convince myself that you were pure evil, I kept thinking about you and your dad. How you actually talk about stuff. I . . . basically I got jealous. And that made it a lot easier to stay mad and not just come to you and tell you what an idiot I'd been. It didn't seem fair that you—"

"We do have something called furniture inside." Rae jerked her head up at the sound of her dad's voice and saw him heading up the front walk toward them. She couldn't believe she hadn't even noticed him drive up. It was just that she'd hardly ever seen Yana like this, all emotional. Despite how angry Rae still was, it was getting to her.

"Maybe you two have heard of it. It's basically padded structures that you can sit on with comfort," Rae's dad continued as he reached them.

"Hi, Mr. Voight," Yana said.

"Hello, Ilyana."

"Ilyana?" Rae echoed, raising her eyebrows.

Mr. Voight flashed a broad grin, and Rae recognized the expression—he'd had one of those good days where his students actually got all the complex stuff he taught.

"Yes, I've decided to start calling her Ilyana," he

replied. He looked back at Yana. "It suits you, I think," he told her, his tone full of that good-mood pep. "Unless you hate it," he added. "Rae threatens me with a long and painful death every time I forget and call her Rachel."

Yana actually blushed. Lea, Rae's old best friend, would have gotten a pained expression on her face and shot Rae a get-me-out-of-here look. But Yana seemed like she could stand there all day. And with Yana's dad the way he was, it kind of made sense.

"No, it's okay," Yana answered, her blush deepening. "No one calls me that. But I like it."

"So are you going to invite us in?" Rae's dad asked.

Rae tried not to wince. "Sure," she answered, backing up and swinging the door all the way open. "Let's go into my room," she said to Yana. She was going to have to listen to the rest of what Yana had to say. But she wasn't going to have the conversation in front of her dad. She jerked her chin in the direction of her bedroom and silently led the way there. "Okay, in a few minutes I'm sure my dad will show up with some lame kind of snack thing for us." Rae shut the door behind Yana. "After that, you leave."

She expected Yana to launch right back into her apologizing slash begging slash explaining. But Yana just sat down in Rae's leather desk chair. It was like a switch had been turned off inside her.

Seeing my dad hurt, Rae realized. She couldn't stop herself from feeling a little squirt of sympathy. *Remember what this girl did to you,* she told herself as she sat down on the bed. She planned to stay as silent as Yana until the snacks arrived. Instead she blurted, "You might as well finish what you were saying. It's better than us sitting here staring at each other."

Yana let out a long sigh but didn't say anything.

"You were telling me how you felt jealous of my dad," Rae prompted.

"Yeah. Shocker, huh?" Yana gave a harsh bark of laughter. "You have this perfect dad, and I have—forget it. I'll leave when you tell me to." She grabbed a copy of *Glamour* off Rae's desk and flipped it open. "Just pretend I'm not here. I shouldn't even have come."

"But you *are* here," Rae said. "Don't try to guilt me out by acting all martyr. It's not you, and we both know it, so—"

There was a thump on Rae's door that sounded like a kick. Rae jumped up and opened the door. Her dad came in with a glass of Coke in each hand and a plate of something chocolate balanced on top of the glasses. Yana stood up and rescued the plate. "Made those myself," Rae's dad bragged.

"Wow," Yana said, staring at the little disks of chocolate with swirls of white icing inside.

Rae's dad leaned close to Yana. "They're Yodels, carefully carved Yodels," he told her in a loud whisper. "Don't tell Rae. She really thinks I bake them." He set the Cokes on Rae's desk. "I'll leave you two alone. I can see when I'm not wanted," he said. Then he left, closing the door behind him.

He must have had a genius in his class today, Rae thought. He was being even loonier than usual. Of course, it also could be because Rae had a friend over for the first time in a while. Maybe he'd been getting worried since Yana and Anthony hadn't been around lately.

"Your dad's kind of funny," Yana commented. She picked up a Yodel slice, studied it, and popped it into her mouth.

"He's just happy that I finally seem mentally stable and actually have a friend," Rae answered. She picked up one of the Cokes and wrapped both hands around it. "So what's your deal? What do you need me to do? I'm not saying I will or anything—but what's going on?"

Yana hesitated.

I'm not going to plead with her to tell me, Rae thought. *I asked her. That's enough. More than enough. God, the girl ripped out my heart with her fingernails.*

But if Yana was in trouble, real trouble . . .

"Just tell me," Rae said, her voice raised.

"I think my dad wants to put me away," Yana burst out.

"What?" Rae squinted at Yana. What was she talking about?

"I caught him talking to one of the doctors from the hospital where you were in the summer," Yana rushed on. "The doctor was actually at my house. At my *house*."

Rae frowned. "Okay, but that doesn't mean he's planning to have you institutionalized," she replied. Just thinking about the hospital made her feel sick and weak, like someone had removed half of her bones and vital organs.

"There were girls in that place who weren't at all crazy, you know that," Yana protested. "Girls whose parents just didn't want to deal."

"But—"

"You're never going to get it," Yana snapped. "Not with a dad like yours. But my father, he's always basically acted like I wasn't even there. And as long as I didn't cause him any problems, that was fine. But now with the letter, and getting called to the principal for a lecture about me skipping school and getting in a fight with this loser girl—it pissed him off."

Yana took a swallow of her Coke and kept on

talking, like now that she'd started, she'd never be able to stop. "Plus his new bimbette hates me. I know she's doing everything she can to convince him to dump me somewhere so the two of them can do their thing with no interruptions. The witch probably put the call in to the doctor herself."

"You're not going to end up in the hospital," Rae said firmly. And she meant it. She couldn't let anyone—even someone who'd completely betrayed her—end up there. Not someone who was totally sane.

"You're going to help me?" Yana asked, her voice cracking.

Rae sighed. "What do you want me to do?" she asked.

Yana's lips lifted slightly to something in the family of a smile. "Thanks," she said. "I figured you could just do your fingerprint thing on something with my dad's fingerprints and tell me that I'm wrong about what he has planned. Or . . . or that I'm right."

Rae nodded. "Fine. But this doesn't mean anything," she warned. "We're not friends. And once I'm done, I'm done. You can't come back here again asking me for something else."

"Understood," Yana said, her blue eyes intense on Rae's face.

* * *

"Jesse!" Anthony called, waving him over to his table at the Chick Filet. Jesse veered toward him, and Anthony could tell he was trying not to smile.

"Wow. Seeing Anthony Fascinelli in person. What a privilege." Jesse sat down and started in on Anthony's curly fries.

Crap. Jesse was right. Anthony'd pretty much disappeared when he was hanging with Yana. Weren't there even a couple of times when Jesse'd left messages and Anthony'd blown them off? And now, just because he needed Jesse's help—again— he expected Jesse to come like a well-trained dog.

"I'm such a jerk," Anthony said, using his fingers to rake his hair off his face. "Look, you're right. I haven't been around much. And then just because I needed help with something. I—" He hesitated but then went on, figuring he owed Jesse the truth. "Yana and I were sort of together for a while, and—"

"Yana, not Rae?" Jesse interrupted.

"Yeah, Yana. Rae, you know, Rae's a friend," Anthony answered. What was Jesse thinking? "Anyway, I guess I got so into her that I forgot about everything else. So, sorry. Sorry I didn't call back those times. I should have said that before."

"Doesn't matter," Jesse said. "But what's the deal? You're not with Yana anymore?"

A hot flush rose up the back of Anthony's neck.

"No, turns out Yana only wanted to be with me to piss Rae off." Anthony jammed his hands in his back pockets. "Anyway, I could use your help again, if you've got time."

"I'm here, right?" Jesse said. He leaned in closer to Anthony. "I was thinking about what you told me on the phone," he said. "Unclean. I don't even get what that's supposed to mean." He ran a curly fry around and around in the pool of ketchup on Anthony's plate until it was completely drenched. Anthony had to look away. The ketchup reminded him too much of the dripping red letters on Rae's locker.

"I don't know what it means exactly, either," Anthony admitted. "But somebody is still after Rae. She thinks she's safe now because that Steve Mercer guy is dead, but she's not. We've gotta figure out what the deal is."

Jesse took another fry off Anthony's plate and started dragging it through the ketchup. "What about the government guys? They were the ones who were behind the experiments. And they killed Mercer. Maybe they aren't happy that Rae knows about them."

"Maybe," Anthony answered. "But painting in fake blood on a locker doesn't seem like their style." He gave a harsh laugh. "Not that I know anything about them. But if you're this high-tech government agency, painting on a locker seems pretty lame."

Jesse raised one eyebrow. "Unless they did it *because* it wouldn't seem like their style. Maybe they're trying to fake Rae out. Make her think that somebody besides them is threatening her."

He sounded so excited. Like this was some live action video game or something. Anthony started to point out to Jesse that they were talking about Rae's life but held back. Jesse knew the stakes. He'd been kidnapped because of his connection to Rae, and even after that he'd never backed off from helping her whenever she needed it.

Anthony dug his knuckles into his forehead, as if that would help him think. "The government people who killed Mercer could have killed Rae right then. But they didn't. They wanted to, but that guy Aiden stopped them."

"So maybe we should be talking to Aiden," Jesse said.

"You're right." Anthony shoved himself to his feet. "Even if Aiden confirms that the government agency wasn't behind the locker thing, maybe he'll have some idea who else would want to threaten Rae."

"So let's go to the Wilton Center. He could be there right now." Jesse stood up, too. "I know the basic layout of the place because Rae and I went in there. She found out that they're still doing experiments on people. Down in the basement."

A jolt of acid entered Anthony's stomach. Jesse had obviously been there for Rae. While Anthony had been sticking his tongue down Yana's throat. Very nice. *Not the time to be thinking about it,* he told himself.

"Jesse, asking a bunch of questions—it might not be exactly healthy, you know. You don't have to come if—"

"Just shut up," Jesse said. He led the way out to the parking lot and over to Anthony's car. He got inside without another word.

Anthony slid behind the wheel and slammed the door. "So I guess we need a cover story," he told Jesse. They talked plans until Anthony pulled into the parking lot of the center. "We're here," he said, like a freakin' idiot. He got out of the car fast and headed toward the center. Jesse fell into place beside him. Together they walked through the double doors. There was a map posted on the wall, and Anthony found the administration office on it. He and Jesse immediately headed for it.

"Can I help—" the woman behind the desk began as soon as they stepped through the door.

Jesse smiled. "Hey, my brother brought me here to sign me up for a woodworking class. I want to make a skateboard. I came up with the design myself."

Enough, Anthony thought. But the woman seemed

to be liking Jesse's enthusiasm. "We're supposed to talk to Aiden Matthews," Anthony added, trying to keep them on track.

The woman twined one long section of her dark hair around her finger, and Anthony noticed that the black had a streak of deep purple in it. "I'm sure we have a class for you," she told Jesse, then her eyes flicked to Anthony. "But Aiden Matthews isn't with the center anymore."

"Really?" Anthony asked. "I just talked to him a few days ago."

"It was a sudden decision," the woman answered, unrolling her hair from her finger. "He, um, he found a job elsewhere." She began rerolling the hair as soon as she had it completely loose. *Nervous much?* Anthony thought.

"Can we get his number?" Jesse asked. "He seemed to really get the skateboard idea I had. Maybe he could, like, do private classes with me. It wouldn't take that many, I don't think."

"Sorry," the woman said. "I can't give out employee—or ex-employee—personal information. But I'm sure that you'll like the wood shop teacher we have. I know he could—"

"I need some juice," Jesse interrupted.

Anthony unzipped his backpack and pretended to search through it. "Crap. I forgot to put more in." He gave the woman an apologetic smile. "Sorry. It's just, my brother has diabetes. Sometimes he needs juice when his sugar drops too far."

"I passed out one time," Jesse added.

"I'm sure we have some in the kitchen," the woman said.

"That'd be great," Anthony told her, impressed by Jesse's quick thinking. "Could he just sit down and wait? I don't want him standing up until I know he's okay."

"Of course. I'll be back in one minute." The woman rushed out of the room.

"You hear that? One minute." Jesse was already sliding into the seat behind the computer. Anthony headed for the row of gray metal filing cabinets. "Matthews, Matthews," he muttered.

"Already got it," Jesse called out. "Even has a picture of the guy." As soon as the printer spit out the info they needed, they bolted. "So should we find a pay phone?" Jesse asked as soon as they were back in the car.

"I want to go there in person," Anthony answered as he backed out of the parking slot. "I don't want to give him the chance to hang up or something."

"It's at 5002 Carlton," Jesse said. "Do you know how to get there?"

"Yeah, I did some work on a car for a guy who lived pretty near that address," Anthony said. He cranked up the radio and drove as fast as he legally could, his mind filled with images of what he could do to Aiden if he was stupid enough to refuse to talk to them.

Remember that he's the guy who saved Rae, Anthony told himself as he swung onto Aiden's street. *Don't get all crazy on him. Unless you have to.*

"Doesn't look like he's home," Jesse commented as Anthony parked a few houses away.

"Let's check it out," Anthony said, although he was pretty sure Jesse was right. The house was completely dark, and there was no car in the driveway.

Anthony headed up the front walkway, trying to look like he had a very good and proper reason to be there. His gut clenched when he reached the porch. The door stood slightly ajar. Somehow he didn't picture this Aiden guy leaving his door open.

Gently Anthony nudged the door all the way open and stepped inside. His footsteps echoed on the tile hallway. But it didn't matter. The place was empty. Not even a stick of furniture.

"Guess we're not going to be talking to the guy tonight," Jesse said.

Rae stepped into the gym, her arm looped through Marcus's, and her breath caught in her chest. She knew that she hadn't really walked right into the middle of a moonbeam. She knew all she was really seeing was glitter and lighting effects and phosphorescent paint. But for that one moment, it was like magic did exist in the world.

"Hey, Marcus, Rae! Over here," Vince called. His voice broke the spell. Rae was back in the gym, the red lines of the basketball court not completely hidden by the sparkling white confetti and silver balloons strewn across the polished wood floor.

But it's still magic, Rae thought as they headed over to the waiting group of Marcus's friends. *Marcus's and* my *friends,* she corrected herself. *I'm here with the most popular guy in the entire school, a gorgeous guy, a guy who pretty much begged me to be with him. And all the creamy crème de la crème of the school are right there, expecting us to join them. 'Cause we belong. 'Cause I belong. God, if the geeky sixth-grade Rachel could see the high school junior Rae right now, she'd probably scream before she fainted dead away.*

"You guys are late. Did you get, uh, distracted on the way here?" Lea asked. She smiled like she was just being friendly, but there was something underneath the smile, something jealous and ugly. *And we were best friends for four years,* Rae thought. Maybe she and Yana should—no. Rae wasn't going to ruin the night obsessing about Yana or Lea or anything else in the slightest bit unpleasant.

Marcus pulled Rae tight against his side. "I'm always distracted around Rae," he told Lea.

"Where's Jackie tonight?" Rae asked, going for a subject change.

"Her family is jetting off to Tahoe for some skiing," Chris answered. "Maybe I should try downing a bottle of aspirin. A lame suicide attempt and I could be—"

Marcus whacked Chris on the head. "McHugh, what did I tell you about trying to think?"

"That when I feel like attempting it, I should—"

The squeal of a microphone being turned on interrupted him. "Okay, everyone, it's that time," the principal's voice boomed out. "Time to find out who's this year's Moonbeam King and Queen."

"Kill me now," someone behind Rae muttered. A guy, of course. Guys had no appreciation for the fact that electing a Moonbeam King and Queen was a tradition that went back to the very first year Sanderson Prep was founded. And that was back before the Civil War.

"We had to count the votes twice," the principal continued. "It was very close this year. But I'm happy to announce that your king and queen arrrrrre . . ." He paused, grinning at the groans of anticipation that filled the gym. "Arrrre Marcus Salkow and Rae Voight."

"No way!" Rae squealed, sounding exactly like the sixth-grade Rachel.

"Like there was any other choice," Marcus said, grabbing her into a hard hug that quickly transitioned into a long, sweet kiss.

The microphone squealed again, and the principal loudly cleared his throat. "There's a little thing called the spotlight dance that's supposed to be happening," he reminded them.

Marcus reluctantly released Rae. Well, almost

released her. He kept her hand in his and led her over to the spot of perfect white light in the middle of the dance floor. A song began to play. Rae knew it, it was one of her favorites, but she couldn't come up with the name. Her brain was incapable of that kind of thinking. It was incapable of coming up with any words at all. Because she wasn't just inside a moonbeam. She *was* a moonbeam.

It sounded ridiculous, ridiculous and totally cheesy. But her body felt like it was made of glimmering light. She was weightless, insubstantial, unable to feel her feet on the floor. Unable even to feel Marcus's arms around her. Floating. Flying. Free of the earth. She closed her eyes, wanting to hold on to the sensation as long as she could.

Anthony hesitated outside the doors of the gym. The lights were dim inside, and pretty much everyone was in the butt-groping hanging-all-over-each-other stage instead of actually dancing. *Get in there,* he told himself. *You have to tell Rae what's going on, so stop screwing around and get the hell in there.*

The slow song playing segued into another slow song, but Marcus and Rae didn't move apart. They'd danced every dance since Anthony showed up. Obviously if he was going to talk to her, he was going to have to go up and interrupt them. Yeah, go on up, like a total loser.

Anthony forced himself to step into the gym. Little flakes of glittering confetti crunched under his shoes. *I'll probably be picking the crap off myself for weeks,* he thought as he came to a stop next to the punch-and-cookie table that a couple of parents were supervising. Punch and cookies. Man, *so* not a Fillmore High kind of dance. He took a cup of punch from the closest prep-school-mom type, wondering if she could tell that he belonged here about as much as a chicken in a clown suit.

Doesn't matter. How can you even be thinking about bull like that? Anthony asked himself. *You're supposed to be warning Rae, and you're getting all knotted up about whether you fit in okay at a freakin' moon crap dance. Very nice, Fascinelli.*

He took a gulp of his punch, his eyes automatically tracking Rae and Marcus. Marcus's hands were threaded through Rae's curly hair. God, Anthony loved the way her hair felt, so fantastically soft, and thick, and smelling like—

He slammed his punch down on the table. The contents sloshed over the sides, and the mom gave him a disapproving look. *Don't know any better,* Anthony felt like telling her. *I used to go to Fillmore.*

Okay, now do it. No hesitation, he told himself. And he elbowed his way onto the dance floor and directly over to Rae and Marcus. Neither of them noticed him. Rae's eyes were closed, her head resting on Marcus's chest. Marcus's eyes were closed, too. He'd moved his hands down to Rae's waist, and now his cheek was pressed against the top of Rae's head. The guy was way too friggin' tall.

Anthony gave a little cough. Got no reaction. He could probably drag in a wrecking ball and bring the building down around them without getting a reaction. Rae . . . she looked so peaceful. Like there was no place she'd rather be.

"Salkow," Anthony said loudly. He reached out and poked Marcus on the shoulder. Reluctantly Marcus lifted his head and opened his eyes.

"Fascinelli, you came," Marcus exclaimed. Rae's eyes snapped open at Anthony's name, and she broke away from Marcus, stumbling on her high heels.

"Yeah, I decided to come," Anthony answered, feeling the back of his neck flushing. Any second now his pits would start pumping juice.

"Rae and I won Moonbeam King and Queen, even without your vote," Marcus said, looping his arm around Rae, his hand coming to rest way too close to her breast. Well, not that close. But still.

"Uh, good, great," Anthony managed to get out when he realized they were both waiting for some kind of humanoid response from him. "I was wondering, do you think I could maybe dance with the queen?"

Now that, that was subhuman. Extremely. But Marcus just smiled. "How can I say no, after you helped me get Rae back? But only one dance, okay? That's all the time away from her I can stand." He winked at Rae, then let her go and headed toward the guys' bathroom.

"Thanks for asking *me*," Rae muttered as Anthony took a step toward her.

He jerked to a stop. What? Did she not want him to touch her? *Moron, she made it completely clear this morning that she doesn't even want to talk to you.*

"Forget it," Rae said. She stepped up to him and lightly rested her hands on his shoulders. With those heels on, she was actually slightly taller than him, but her eyes were still fixed on his. *What's she thinking?* he wondered. *She keeps staring. What is she thinking?*

"Uh, you're not actually dancing," Rae finally told him. He could feel her warm breath against his face as she spoke.

"Oh. Yeah. Right." Anthony carefully put his hands on her waist, touching as lightly as he could, and started swaying to the music. Not that the music was easy to hear. Anthony's heart was pounding way too loud for the band to compete with. "I went to Aiden Matthews's after practice," he blurted.

"What?" Rae demanded, her eyes as hard as blue steel. "Why'd you do that?"

"Because—" He so did not want to tell her this. But it had to be done. "Because I went by your locker after school, and there was a message on it."

Rae's body stiffened. "From who?" she bit out.

"I don't know," Anthony answered. "It was just one word painted on the door. Unclean." He rushed on, not wanting to give her a lot of time to think about the word. "I thought maybe Aiden would know who might still be wanting to threaten you."

"Unclean," Rae repeated, her voice strained. "Painted on my locker?"

Anthony instinctively tightened his grip around her. "I cleaned it off," he said. "It's gone. But Rae, whoever did that—"

"It's not really a threat," she jumped in. "I mean, unclean, what does that even mean, anyway?"

Anthony frowned. Rae had to take this seriously. How could she not? "I don't know," he admitted. "That's one of the things I was going to ask Aiden. But when I showed up, he was gone. Moved out. No forwarding address. It's interesting that he made the move right after he yanked the government guys off you."

Rae's hands tightened into fists, bunching up his shirt under her fingers. "And it's supposed to be my fault, Anthony? God, maybe he wanted a bigger place. Maybe he moved in with his girlfriend."

"Maybe," Anthony answered. But he couldn't back off this, no matter how much she wanted him to. "But with the timing thing, maybe not. I came over here because I think you need to be extra careful until we figure out what Aiden's deal is. Somebody is still trying to scare you. At *least* scare you. And without Aiden to put a stop—"

"Look, I know the government goons are always going to be watching me. That's a given. I'm sure the locker thing was just a little reminder of that," Rae shot back. "Maybe they even suspect that I told you the truth about them. That's something they definitely wouldn't want. So maybe they decided to do something small. Like I said, just to remind me to stay in line. That's fine—I plan on forgetting about this whole thing, anyway."

"I'm not so sure," Anthony began. "Maybe it is a little warning from the government guys. But it seems pretty lame for them, don't you think? Painting on a locker—would that really be their style?"

"The agency guys are the only ones who could be responsible," Rae insisted. "There's definitely not anyone else interested in me that way. They probably . . . they probably wanted to send me a message in a way that would look basically normal. Paint on a locker—that's normal in a high school." Rae pulled away from him. "And you know what? It's not anything you have to worry about anymore." She glanced over her shoulder. "Marcus is waiting for me."

"Rae, you—"

She cut him off again. "Have a nice life, Anthony." The words were like the blows of a baseball bat to the back of his head. It took him a moment to realize that she'd turned around and was walking away from him.

Anthony stared after her, unable to move. It wasn't like he'd wanted her to be terrified. But Rae pretending that everything was okay was dangerous. It could even be deadly.

Marcus reached across the seat and gently pulled a piece of shiny confetti out of Rae's hair. "For your scrapbook," he said as he handed it to her.

"Huh?" Rae asked. "Oh, yeah, my scrapbook." She'd totally forgotten about it. How bizarre was that? Less than a year ago the scrapbook had been like some kind of religious artifact. It had mementos from every date they'd been on. It even had the wrapper from the straw he'd been using the first time he talked to her in the caf. Rae grabbed her purse off the floor, getting no thoughts through her wax-coated fingertips, and put the confetti in the little inside pocket.

"Did you have fun tonight?" Marcus asked.

"Of course. Yeah. It was fabulous," Rae answered. And it had been. Until Anthony showed up. After that, hard as she tried, Rae'd never been able to completely relax. *Forget what he said,* she ordered herself for the millionth time. *He was being a drama queen. Don't let him spoil your first real back-together night with Marcus. This is the best part, remember?* She'd always loved sitting with Marcus, parked on her quiet street. She felt the closest to him then, like the car was their own private little world.

Rae took Marcus's face in her hands. Slowly, slowly, trying to savor every detail, she lowered her lips to his and kissed him. He tasted like lime punch and breath mints. *Not exactly the best combo,* she thought.

This is not a taste test, she told herself. She kissed him again, just his top lip. Then gave equal attention to his bottom lip—she loved his bottom lip, the way it was just a little bit fuller than the top.

Marcus gave a sound that was half groan and half whimper. *He's really getting into this,* she realized. And she . . . she was, too. Kissing Marcus was always amazing. It's just that they'd been kissing so much at the dance, so it made sense that this kissing wasn't quite as exciting as usual. It was like she was on kissing overload. Her senses were numbed out from too much use.

Except when you danced with Anthony. The thought zipped through her head like an annoying fly. But she couldn't deny that it was true. Just the feel of Anthony's hands on her waist had lit up every nerve in her body. And her veins had felt like they were shooting electricity instead of blood.

Just a freak physical response, she decided. *It's not about Anthony, it's just about . . . about . . .*

This is not the time for thinking, Rae told herself. She slid her arms around Marcus's neck, then kissed him again, her lips open against his.

God, that minty lime taste was icky. That's why she wasn't responding the way she had to Anthony. It would be impossible while tasting that combo.

Marcus had probably popped the mints for the parked-in-the-car make-out session. He was trying to be thoughtful. But yuck.

Rae buried her head against Marcus's chest. Yeah, that was better. Warm. Comfy. She could fall asleep right here. That was how right it felt to be cuddled up with Marcus.

Marcus kissed the top of her head. Then her forehead. Then he leaned down far enough to kiss her nose. The lips would be next. Rae didn't want to offend him by seeming lukewarm. Better to make a break for it. She'd kiss him triple next time she saw him, when that taste was gone.

"I should go in. My dad's still kind of in overprotective mode," Rae said.

Marcus frowned. "Okay, I guess I can let you go," he teased, tracing the line of her jaw with his fingers.

"Thanks for—thanks for tonight," Rae said quickly. She leaned over and gave Marcus a fast kiss on the cheek, then got out of the car before he had the chance to coax her into a few more minutes.

"Keys, keys, need keys," she muttered as she crossed the front lawn, listening to the sound of Marcus's car taking off down the street. She stood on the porch, digging through her purse, feeling for the cool metal. As she took a step closer to the front door, the automatic porch light came on and she finally found the keys.

"Got them." She pulled her key ring free and went to unlock the door.

The keys fell out of her suddenly nerveless hand as she saw the front door clearly now that it was bathed in harsh light. This wasn't possible. Not here, not on her own front door. *Her dad's house.*

Her hands shaking, Rae bent down to pick up the keys. Then she stood, staring at the door, unable to put the key in the lock.

Unclean. The word *unclean* had been written across the door in blood-colored paint.

Anthony was right, Rae thought, shivers running through her whole body.

No! No. I was right, she screamed inwardly. *This is just a reminder that I'm being watched. And that I need to keep my mouth shut. That I have to stay in line.*

And she could deal with that. No problem at all. She'd clean the words off her door before her dad saw the message, and then just keep being normal Rae. She would spend her whole life staying in line if that's what it took. But she wasn't going to let these people ruin her life—or hurt anyone else she cared about.

*   *   *

You're not quite so happy now, are you, Rae? And I'm a little happier. Especially because this is it. You've reached the final days. Too bad you won't enjoy them. I plan to make you as miserable as possible before I kill you. You deserve that. I deserve that. My mother deserves that.

Chapter 4

Rae waved to her father as he pulled out of Yana's driveway Saturday morning. *God, I really have to get my license,* she thought. *I'm sixteen now. Way too old to be driven around by daddy.*

Now that my life is settling down—as long as I'm the good girl the government people want me to be—I can start doing normal stuff again. Like getting ready to take my driver's test.

Rae realized she was still standing in Yana's driveway. Stalling. She sucked in a deep breath and started up the walkway to Yana's house. The blooms on the plants Yana had grown on either side of the walkway were gone, and the stems looked kind of sad and naked with just the leaves. "I can't believe

I'm doing this," she muttered as she reached the door. "I mean, there's nice, and then there's doormat." Rae reached out and rang the doorbell, anyway. All she had to do was a quick fingerprint sweep, then she'd be outta there.

"Hi," Yana said as she swung open the door. "Hi," she repeated. "Come on in. I'm making us waffles. Blueberry ones," Yana added over her shoulder as she led the way into the kitchen.

Rae followed, feeling strange about finally being in Yana's house. It was almost like she'd expected the place to be obviously different somehow, the way Yana had been so weird about not letting her come inside before. But no—it was a house. Normal enough.

"Wait," Rae said as she spotted a mixing bowl on the kitchen counter. "You're actually *making* waffles," she demanded. "I thought you meant you were taking some Eggos out of the freezer and putting them in the toaster."

"Nope," Yana answered. She spooned some of the batter into a waffle iron. *A waffle iron.* Rae hadn't even known anyone actually had waffle irons anymore. She'd thought they were all in museums. She'd definitely never thought she'd see Yana Savari using one.

Except . . . except Yana had done the gardening

thing in the front yard. And God, it looked like the cushions on the folding chairs positioned around the kitchen table were homemade. "So are you going to sit down or what?" Yana asked as the waffle batter sizzled.

"Sure." Rae sat down in the closest chair, even though she didn't want to. She didn't want to eat the yummy-smelling waffles, either. What she wanted was to do what she'd come here to do. Period. What was Yana doing making waffles for her, anyway? Why would she possibly think that Rae'd want to eat waffles with the person who'd gone behind her back and taken her boyfriend? Okay, not her boyfriend. But the guy who had kissed her in a way that only a guy who was her boyfriend should.

"You know what?" Rae asked. "I'm not really hungry. Can you just get me something of your dad's? It would be good if it was something he touched near the time that he was talking to the doctor who was—"

"Not so loud, okay? He's home," Yana muttered.

"Oh." Rae hadn't even thought of that possibility. She'd never met Yana's dad. Which wasn't that strange, considering she'd never been inside Yana's house before. "What I was going to say is that it would be good if you could get me something your dad would have touched really soon after he talked to the doctor," Rae whispered. "That's when there'd be the best chance he was thinking about you so I could pick up some useful stuff."

"So forget the waffles," Yana said.

"Yeah, forget them," Rae replied, ignoring the thin vein of hurt she'd heard in Yana's voice. Like refusing a waffle was anywhere close to what Yana had done to Rae.

"Do you want juice? I made juice. With oranges," Yana said.

Can't you tell I just want to get out of here? That I don't want to spend one second more in your presence than I have to? Rae wanted to scream. But what came out of her mouth was a quiet, "Okay, sure, orange juice."

You are such a weenie, Rae told herself. *Just because Yana is doing the breakfast thing to try and make you forgive her doesn't mean you have to go along with it.*

Yana went to the cupboard, took out a glass, using the tips of her fingers on one hand and just the palm of her other hand. *Gee, wonder why?* Rae thought. She casually ran her fingers over the tabletop. Yeah, Yana'd wiped it. Clearly it was only Yana's dad's thoughts that Rae was supposed to go digging into. *Thanks for trusting me, Yana. You should know that I wouldn't—*

A high-pitched screeching sound filled the kitchen. Yana dropped the glass, and it shattered on the tile floor. "Crap. Just crap," Yana burst out. She grabbed the dish towel that was looped over the faucet of the kitchen sink, then jerked a chair into position under the screeching smoke detector and started flapping the towel at it. "Can you get the waffles?"

Rae stumbled to her feet and hurried over to the waffle iron. Tendrils of smoke were sneaking out the sides. Rae yanked the plug. Would it help to open the iron, or would more smoke—

"What in the hell is going on out there?" a man yelled. "Jeanette and I are trying to sleep."

"Crap," Yana said again. She jerked the cover of the smoke detector, yanked out the batteries, and threw them on the floor. They bounced near the feet of the man who had just walked into the kitchen.

Rae turned toward him and put on her best meeting-the-parents smile. But the man ignored her. "Jeanette was working until two last night," he snapped. "She doesn't need this."

"It's not like I planned it," Yana muttered. She jumped off the chair.

"Don't get smart," her father warned. He scrubbed his hands through his sandy brown hair and hitched up his sweatpants. "Did you make coffee, at least?"

"Don't I always?" Yana asked. She didn't even glance in Rae's direction. Forget about trying to make an introduction. *Although maybe that's a good thing,* Rae thought. Yana's dad didn't look like he'd be happy to meet anyone right now. Unlike Rae's dad. Who practically leapt around with joy whenever she brought someone home. Yeah, it was partly because it was proof that she was approaching normalcy again. But even before the incident, even before Rae spent the summer in the mental hospital, her dad had always been the dad that drove her and her friends places. He'd even been assistant leader of her Brownie troop.

Yana's dad took two steps toward the coffeemaker, then let out a string of curses that wouldn't quit. "There's glass all over the damn floor, Yana," he said as he sat down in the closest chair.

"Want me to get some peroxide?" Yana volunteered.

"I want you to clean up this sty, that's what I want. And do it by the time Jeanette and I get up." He dug around in the bottom of his foot, found a sliver of glass, and pulled it out. Then he licked his finger and rubbed the bleeding spot.

"You should clean that or—" Yana began.

"I'm going back to bed. Keep it down." Yana's dad got up and left the kitchen.

"Ladies and gentlemen, my father," Yana said after a door shut somewhere down the hall.

Rae thought about trying to make a joke. But she couldn't think of anything even a little bit funny.

"Is there still enough waffle stuff?" she asked softly. "I'm starving, suddenly."

"Now you're hungry," Yana complained, but there was definitely a note of happiness in her voice. Rae couldn't help feeling that little twinge of sympathy for Yana growing bigger by the second.

"Yeah, now I'm hungry," Rae answered. She got up and grabbed a broom from beside the fridge.

"You sure you know how to use one of those things?" Yana asked as she dumped the burned waffles into the garbage. "I know you have a house-keeper and everything."

Rae felt a splotch of guilt start growing on the wall of her stomach. *Oh, come on,* she told herself. *It's not your fault that you have it better than Yana. It's not like you have a decent dad and a house-keeper just to make her feel bad.* Rae flipped the broom over and poked at the glass on the floor with the handle. "Like this, right?" she asked Yana. And she actually got a smile. And she actually cared that she got a smile. Because she was a weenie.

"Hey, Yan," Rae said as she started sweeping with the right end of the broom.

"Huh?" Yana finished wiping out the waffle iron

and plugged it in. "I said huh," she added when Rae didn't go on.

"We never talked about this. But I was wondering." Rae hesitated. "I was wondering what the story is on your mom."

"Don't go there, okay?" Yana snatched up the mixing bowl and started to spoon batter onto the waffle iron.

Her hands are shaking, Rae noticed.

"My dad and me—it's the one thing we agree on. We don't talk about her. Ever. Not after what she did to us."

Rae nodded. Did Yana's mom leave them? Did she find another guy or something? More and more questions circled her brain, but she didn't speak any of them aloud. She was afraid Yana would explode into a million pieces if she did.

"I'll go get something of my dad's," Yana announced. She slammed down the lid of the waffle iron and bolted. Rae found the dustpan and swept up her little pile of glass. Then she put the dustpan and broom back where she'd found them. Yana seemed pretty big on keeping things neat. *I wonder if her dad even realizes that,* Rae wondered. *Or does he think the place stays clean by itself? And those flowers out front—does he think they just happened to grow in perfect lines on both sides of the walkway?*

"Here," Yana said as she came back into the kitchen. "My dad always uses this hand-strengthener thing when he's angry. And he was definitely angry after he talked to the doctor from the hospital."

Rae took the strengthening device off Yana's open palms. She ran the fingers of her right hand over the rubber grips.

Hot blood flooded into the veins and arteries of her head. Too much. Too much. They were going to burst. Rae heard a low groan of pain, and it took her a moment to realize it was coming from her own throat.

/Jeanette wants/no good/hospital/wild/crappy pay/Yana has to go/Jeanette says/doctor can commit/by ourselves/

The blood in Rae's brain turned hotter. Scalding and sizzling. *Drop it. Just drop the freakin' thing.* She forced her fingers to uncurl from around the rubber grip. The hand strengthener fell to the floor. Rae sat down beside it.

"Are you okay? What happened?" Yana knelt next to Rae and lightly rested her hand on Rae's shoulder.

"I'm okay. I'm okay," Rae said breathlessly. She forced herself to meet Yana's gaze. "You were right. Don't worry. I'll help you. I promise." She felt her eyes fill with pity as she looked at Yana. "Yan, your dad does want to get you institutionalized."

* * *

The front door to Aiden Matthews's house was still unlocked. Anthony stepped inside, trying to ignore the fact that the sound of his footsteps in the empty hallway gave him the creeps. Because what was he—six years old?

He opened the closet door. A few metal hangers hung on the clothes rack, but that was it. He slammed the door. Rae should be here. Who knew what kind of fingerprint info could be in what looked like an empty closet? But no, Rae was way too busy to be worrying about the fact that her friggin' life was in danger. Why think about something like that when she could be making out with blond-headed prep-school friggin' god Marcus Salkow? He'd actually heard some girl call Salkow that. A god.

Anthony continued into the living room. Nothing in there except some little dents in the carpet where the furniture used to be and a cleaner square on the wall where a picture used to hang. Suddenly Anthony felt like running over and slamming his fist into that pale square. But he didn't. He shoved his hands in his pockets instead. Why? Because it had finally sunk into the pile of meat that was his head that slamming your fists into stuff when you were pissed only made you more pissed. At first the pain made you forget everything else, but before too long, you were totally pissed off at whatever you were pissed off about and also pissed off at yourself. "Ms. Abramson would be so proud," he muttered. "That's a very good realization, Anthony," he added in a high voice that actually didn't sound that much like Abramson.

Guess I can take impressionists off my list of possible career choices, he thought. That and private detective, he decided as he headed into the cleaned-out bathroom. Although maybe not even the best PI would be able to find any way to track down Aiden in a place this empty. There wasn't a sliver of soap in the shower. There wasn't even an empty toilet paper roll left on the back of the john.

Still the bedroom and the kitchen to go, he reminded himself. Although it almost seemed pointless to bother checking them out. Aiden had obviously been ultracareful about not leaving the tiniest clue behind. If it *had* been Aiden who did the cleanup job. It didn't seem like he'd have left the door unlocked after going to all this trouble. Had someone yanked him out of here, then hauled everything out? Had someone else come in to search the place before Anthony came in the first time and left the door unlocked? Was it the other searcher—if there was one—who'd taken the last piece of toilet paper?

Whoever it was had done a hell of a job. The

only thing in the bedroom was a spiderweb in one corner of the ceiling. The kitchen was just as useless. Not even a drop of water in the sink or a cracker crumb on the counter. *I'm surprised they didn't pull the phone off the wall,* Anthony thought as he headed back toward the front door.

An idea speared into his head just as he was turning the doorknob. Anthony spun around and hauled butt back into the kitchen. *Let this work. This has gotta work,* he thought. He grabbed the phone and pressed redial. He smiled as he heard the little beeps that told him the phone was dialing. His smile became a grin when he heard the way the person on the other end of the phone answered.

I may just have you, Aiden, he thought. *You didn't leave me much, but whether you know it or not, you did leave me something.*

Rae stared at the hospital. It looked like such a nice place, the paint a light, warm yellow instead of sterile white, the front lawn a wide stretch of grass so green and perfect, it wouldn't be out of place on a ritzy golf course. But this was the place Rae had spent the worst months of her life. Just looking at it dried up all the saliva in her mouth and increased the pace of her heartbeat.

"Uh, we're here," Yana said. And Rae realized

that Yana had already gotten out of the car. *Not even back inside and I'm already acting like Queen of the Walnut Farm,* Rae thought, a hot, painful blush spreading up her neck. She scrambled out of the Bug so fast that she slammed her elbow on the side of the door, causing tears to spring to her eyes. Rae blinked them away fast as she slammed the car door, then she shot a look at Yana. Had Yana seen Rae's eyes get all weepy? Did she think it was because—

Yana has her own problems, Rae reminded herself. *And those problems—they are why you're here. This visit has nothing to do with you, so get a grip.*

"I hear you can score some really good drugs here," Rae joked as they headed up the quaint cobblestone path—probably carefully chosen to make patients' families think of a charming hotel instead of a very expensive mental hospital.

"Really? Maybe I should be trying to get in instead of stay out," Yana joked back. But she sounded as freaked as Rae felt. Well, why wouldn't she? Yana knew exactly what it was like to be a patient here. Or almost exactly. She'd never actually been a patient here, but she'd done community service here, community service assigned by the court after some underage-drinking debacle. So she knew about the restraints, the ice baths, the bathrooms without doors. She knew enough to be terrified.

Which was why even though both of them had made jokey little comments, neither of them was laughing as they stepped inside the hospital. Rae got her first nose-hair-burning whiff of the pine-scented industrial-strength cleaner that filled the air.

There is absolutely nothing humorous about this place, she thought. *It's a hellhole. Yeah, the doctors and the nurses and everybody are okay. But it's still a hellhole.* Which was why, no matter what Yana had done, Rae had to keep her from ending up here.

"I guess we should go straight to Dr. Hachin's office if we can," Yana said. She picked up her pace and led the way toward the elevators without stopping at the reception desk.

"Excuse me," the guy at the desk called out. "I need you two to sign in."

"I don't know him. Do you?" Yana whispered as they turned around.

Rae shook her head. "Sorry," she told the guy when it didn't seem like Yana was going to say anything. "My friend used to volunteer here. She's used to going straight in." *Maybe that tidbit will make it a little easier for us to move around without supervision,* Rae thought.

"Really? I'm a volunteer myself," the guy answered.

Rae lowered her voice. "Community service?" she asked as Yana signed them in.

The guy frowned, a prissy little frown. "No, grad school assignment."

Nice work, Rae, she thought.

"Who are you here to see?" the guy asked.

"Samantha Todd. One of the nurses," Yana said quickly. Quickly enough that Rae didn't have the chance to possibly squeeze her foot into her mouth again.

"I'll buzz her," the guy said, punching an extension into the phone. "Yana Savari is here," he said, getting Yana's name off the sign-in sheet. "For Samantha." He listened for a moment, then hung up. "She'll be down in a few when she gets a moment," the guy said. "She wasn't expecting you."

"Do you think he was expecting the bug that has clearly crawled up his behind?" Yana asked as they walked over to the big padded chairs along the wall across from the desk.

"I think he sent it an invitation," Rae answered. Yana gave a snort of laughter as they settled into chairs. Which made Rae giggle. Which made them both completely crack up. *God, that felt good,* Rae thought when she managed to get control of herself. Even here, in the fringes of hell, laughing like that felt good. No one could make Rae laugh the way Yana could.

Which made what Yana'd done so much worse.

How could you laugh with someone? Shop with them? Trade secrets? And then stab them in the back and pour lemon juice and salt into the gaping wound? Because what else would you call Yana showing up with Anthony as her boyfriend at Rae's *sixteenth-birthday dinner?*

"You're thinking about Anthony—about me and Anthony, aren't you?" Yana asked, casting a glance at Rae's expression.

Rae had never been able to hide what she was thinking from anyone. Kind of ironic, considering.

She could lie. But what was the point? "Yeah, I was," she admitted. "I think about it a lot."

Yana scooted closer to Rae. "I know I'm never going to be able to make it up to you, but—"

"Yana! And Rae, too! This is great." Samantha Todd rushed over to Rae and Yana. "I didn't know you guys kept in touch." She gave Yana a quick hug, then moved on to Rae. Rae liked Samantha and everything, but all she could think about was Samantha's hands handing her medication. The taste of the medication suddenly filled her mouth. Sweet, but then bitter. The sugar coating never lasted long enough for the pill to get all the way down. And the noxious aftertaste lasted the whole day.

"You look great," Samantha told Rae when she released her.

"So do you," Rae answered automatically. Maybe that wasn't the right response. Maybe it was supposed to be a given that Samantha would look great. Samantha wasn't the returning nutcase, after all.

Stop it, okay? Rae told herself. *You don't need to be analyzing everything you say. No one else is. There's no chart Samantha is going to be filling out later. Nothing you do today is going to get thrown in your face by some doctor.*

RAE SHOULD NEVER HAVE BEEN RELEASED. SHE SHOULD STILL BE ON MEDS. I CAN SEE IT IN HER EYES.

Where . . . where did those thoughts come from? They sounded like something Samantha could be thinking. But Rae wasn't touching one of Samantha's fingerprints. Rae glanced down at her fingers. She wasn't touching *anything.*

Just forget it, Rae told herself. It was one of those mind burps, the kind that happened when you were really tense. She had to relax. Rae locked her hands behind her back tight enough that her nails dug into her skin. She could feel little half-moons of pain on the backs of her hands, and the pain pulled her out of her panic attack. At least enough so that she could smile at Samantha and give a decent impression of a sane person.

Yana was talking. *Okay, so listen to her. That's*

what a normal person would be doing right now,
Rae coached herself.

". . . we'd go upstairs and visit," Yana concluded.

*RAE SHOULDN'T BE VISITING. SHE SHOULD BE
CHECKING IN. I SHOULD GO CALL HER FATHER AND
TELL HIM THAT.*

Oh my God. Oh my God. Rae's breath caught in her
chest, and it took all her concentration to remember
how to exhale. But she did it, then pulled in another
breath. *In, out, in, out. You can do this,* she thought as
she followed Samantha and Yana over to the elevators.
One or both of them had said something more, something after Yana had mentioned the go-upstairs-and-
visit thing. But Rae had no idea what. *Got to stay
focused,* she ordered herself. *Got to be able to respond
like a human.* So why was she losing it? Why did she
feel like she was about to break down?

There was a ding, and the closest elevator opened.
"So, anything new, Rae? How's your dad? Still teaching at the U?" Samantha asked as she ushered Yana
and Rae into the elevator.

*I SHOULD CALL HIM. HE NEEDS TO KNOW THAT THERE
IS STILL SOMETHING WRONG WITH HER. BAD WRONG.*

Answer her! Rae screamed at herself. *She's
already thinking there's something up. Answer her!*
But what was the word she was looking for? It was
at the tip of her tongue. It was itching in her brain.

72

But she couldn't quite get it. *I have to answer,* she thought, a trickle of sweat slithering down her spine.

"Yes!" she blurted. That's the word she'd been looking for. Such a teeny, tiny, ridiculous little word. "Yes," she repeated. "He's still teaching his medieval literature." *There. There. I got out a hard word. Medieval. That should make it okay. That should show that I'm okay.*

The elevator came to a stop with another ding, and Rae stepped out, out onto her old ward.

MAYBE AN ICE BATH WOULD HELP RAE. OR A SEDATIVE. SHE'S TEETERING. I NEED TO GET HER ADMITTED ASAP.

"No!" Rae exclaimed, the sweat gluing her silk shirt to her back now. Yana and Samantha both turned and looked at her. *Now I'm answering the voice in my head,* Rae thought frantically. That was the worst possible, most stupid—

Damage control, she told herself. *Go to damage control.* "And, um, no, nothing's really new," Rae said, forcing a smile that probably came off like one of the Joker's classic grins. The Joker. Crazy. Insane.

"Well, I guess it hasn't really been that long," Samantha said. "Although I imagine it would feel like forever ago to you."

"Sam, we need you in room seventeen for a minute," another nurse—the one who had examined the contents of Rae's luggage on her very first day—called.

Does she think I'm still crazy, too? Rae wondered. *Can she see it in me?* It didn't look like she did. She followed Samantha down the hall without a backward glance.

"Be right back, you two," Samantha said over her shoulder.

I'LL GET RAE CHECKED IN WHEN I GET BACK. I WON'T LET HER LEAVE.

I should just run, Rae thought. *Maybe I could make it before—*

She pressed her fingers against her throbbing forehead. *You're not picking up thoughts,* she reminded herself. *You're just having some kind of stress freak-out being back in this place. And that's actually totally normal. If it felt okay to be back in here,* that *would be crazy.*

"You all right?" Yana asked.

"Yeah," Rae answered. She and Yana were getting a little bit closer again. But there was no way Rae was spilling her guts to Yana. Not after what she'd done.

"Then let's get going. This might be our only chance to get into Dr. Hachin's office." Yana grabbed Rae's arm and tugged her down the hall in the opposite direction from Samantha and the other nurse.

She came to a halt near an open doorway, then slowly backed away from it, pulling Rae with her. "She's in there," Yana whispered. "If I get her out, will you be okay going in alone?"

"Uh-huh. Definitely," Rae answered. Even though she couldn't say definitely that she'd be able to walk from where she stood to Dr. Hachin's office by herself.

"Go in the visitors' bathroom for a minute. I won't need more than that," Yana instructed.

Left foot, right foot, left foot, right foot. Breathe in, breathe out, breathe in, breathe out. It felt like it took a full hour, but Rae was able to make it to the end of the hall, around the corner, and into the bathroom. She locked the door behind her and leaned against it. Immediately she began to count. "One, one thousand, two, one thousand, three, one thousand." She didn't want time to think. Or to get any of the not-me thoughts—wherever they were coming from.

When she got to sixty, one thousand, Rae right-foot, left-footed back into the hallway and back down to Dr. Hachin's office. She paused outside the open door and listened. "Sounds empty," she whispered, then she stepped inside. "Okay," she said. "I need to touch something that Dr. Hachin would have touched when she was thinking about Yana." Somehow speaking out loud made Rae feel a little calmer.

She scanned the office, and her eyes came to rest on the row of bright green filing cabinets behind Dr. Hachin's orange desk. Dr. Hachin believed in color. Rae remembered how the doctor had made her dad bring her a bright pink sweater for Rae to wear in the hospital, a sweater Rae had ceremoniously burned when she was allowed to go home.

Maybe I shouldn't have burned it. Maybe I'll be needing it again.

"No," she said aloud. "I'm not crazy. I wasn't crazy then. I just didn't know I was a fingerprint reader, so I *thought* I was going crazy when I got the not-me thoughts."

Rae tried to shove away the nagging worry that the thoughts she'd been getting today *hadn't* been coming from fingerprints. She just wasn't going to go there.

"Focus on what you're supposed to be doing. You don't know how long Dr. Hachin will be gone," Rae mumbled to herself.

Finally she found the *S* drawer and pulled it open.
/maybe I should try/ chipped a/ the sister is/

It wasn't just that the thoughts hadn't come from fingerprints, though. She hadn't been touching *anything*.

"Just keep looking," she told herself through clenched teeth as she continued to flip through files.

Wait. There was a file for Yana in here. A thin file in a new-looking folder. Rae slid it free.

/ erratic behavior/ father extremely/ family history/

This was looking bad. It was looking very bad. Rae opened the folder. Inside was a single sheet of paper with a notation of a time and date for an evaluation of Yana Savari.

"What?"

Rae jerked her head up and saw Yana in the doorway. Her face was pale. "What?" she repeated.

"It's not good," Rae admitted. She swept her fingers over the memo.

/ possible manic depressive/ father fears/ erratic/

"Tell me," Yana demanded.

Rae's head was pounding so loudly, it almost drowned out Yana's voice. "You're scheduled for an evaluation," she answered. "And it seems like your dad has been doing whatever he can to make Dr. Hachin think—"

"That I should be put away," Yana finished.

NO, YOU SHOULD BE PUT AWAY, RAE. I CAN SEE THE INSANITY BUBBLING UP INSIDE YOU.

Rae snatched her fingers away from the sheet of paper as if it were on fire. But the thoughts kept coming.

YOU NEED TO BE BACK HERE. SAFE IN YOUR OWN LITTLE ROOM. STRAPPED IN YOUR OWN LITTLE BED.

Those thoughts aren't coming from fingerprints, Rae thought. *And they aren't coming from me. They* aren't.

But wasn't that what all lunatics thought? That the voices in their heads were from God or dogs or aliens or something?

Have I been crazy all this time? Am I going to end up in here for the rest of my life? Rae was sure those thoughts were her own. And they froze the blood in her veins.

Chapter 5

There have to be forty TVs in here, Anthony
thought as he stepped into the dark interior of
The Score. And who knew how many guys—
the place was filled with mostly guys, guys and
waitresses—sitting around drinking and staring at
the screens. He took a quick glance at the photo of
Aiden Matthews that Jesse had pulled out of the
Wilton Center computer, then started to circle the
perimeter of the sports bar, slowly, methodically,
checking out the face of every warm body in the
place. Even if Aiden was disguised in a wig and one
of the tight little referee outfits the waitresses had
on, Anthony was gonna find him.

He let out a disgusted snort when he'd completed
the circuit. He'd found a big fat nothing. *What were*

you expecting? he asked himself. *Did you really think just because the last call Aiden made was to this place that he'd just be sitting here waiting for you?*

Well, yeah, actually that's exactly what Anthony had been thinking. Or at least hoping. If this was some lame detective TV show, Aiden would have been here. *Okay, bartender,* Anthony thought. He headed over to the bar, slid onto an empty stool, and checked out the game on the closest TV. The bartender's eyes were on the game, too, and he seemed in no hurry to take Anthony's order. But when the quarterback fumbled, the guy managed to do his frickin' job and ask what Anthony wanted.

"Beer," Anthony told him, ready to reach for the fake ID he'd gotten in New Orleans. But the bartender dude's attention was back on the game. He slid a draft in front of Anthony without even raising an eyebrow.

A waitress with a braid that reached almost to her butt pushed her way up to the bar. "I need three Buds," she called to the guy behind the bar. He didn't even blink, just kept staring at the game.

"Would you reach over and smack him for me?" the waitress asked Anthony. "I can't reach."

"I heard you, I heard you," the bartender said

before Anthony could respond. He grabbed the beers and pushed them in the direction of the waitress.

"Butt head," she muttered as she slid the beers onto a tray. The bartender didn't respond. Big surprise.

Clearly I'm not going to get any info out of him until a commercial, Anthony thought. He took a sip of his beer, figuring he'd nurse the thing for as long as he had to to stay in the bar. Today was not the day to get hammered. He had to figure out who was still after Rae—government or not government. Not that she cared. The game on the TV wavered, and for a second the screen was filled with the image of Rae kissing Marcus. Kissing him in a way that was making Marcus groan.

Anthony tightened his grip on his beer stein and ordered himself to stop being a moron. He was the one who'd wanted Rae to get back together with Salkow. They belonged together—two purebred poodles. After graduation they'd go off to some big whoop college together, then they'd get married, and Rae'd squeeze out some more little purebreds and everybody would be very happy. As long as Anthony made sure Rae stayed alive to enjoy her perfect life with perfect Marcus, who'd probably be some lawyer or something and make millions every year.

"Can you shove over the pretzels?" Anthony asked the big beer-bellied guy next to him. Beer Belly sent them Anthony's way without taking his eyes off the game. Anthony jammed a fistful of the extra-salty pretzels in his mouth and forced his gaze onto the game, too. No more thinking about Rae. Except telling himself not to think about her was thinking about her, and it made him think about her even more. Crap.

Finally a commercial came on. Every guy sitting at the bar started calling for another round. Anthony waited until the bartender set them all up, then Anthony stuck the photo of Aiden in the guy's face. "Seen him around?" he asked.

The game started back up. "Don't think so," the bartender answered, his head already swiveling back toward the tube.

"Can you take another look?" Anthony asked, trying to keep the irritation out of his voice. The bartender didn't seem like the kind of guy who would respond to being pushed.

"I told you, don't know the guy," the bartender answered without turning back to Anthony.

The waitress with the braid slid between Anthony and Beer Belly's stools. "I need two boilermakers and, if you can believe it, a mint julep," she told the bartender.

"Hey, do you know this guy?" Anthony asked, flashing the picture of Aiden. *Chicks like hearing the details,* he reminded himself. "He's my uncle. My aunt sent me to fetch him home. Family dinner nightmare," he added.

"He hasn't been in today," the waitress said. She grabbed the bar with both hands and hauled herself up on it. Then she smacked the bartender on the head.

"Boilermakers, right," he said.

"And a mint julep," the waitress told him as she slid back to the ground. "But your uncle does come in here a lot. Great tipper," she told Anthony. She lowered her voice. "Gambles a lot. You should talk to that guy over there, the one in the pink shirt. He takes the bets."

"Thanks," Anthony said. He stood up, grabbed his beer, then headed over to the man in pink, who was sitting at a big table in front of a TV showing a horse race. Anthony didn't know which one. Not his thing. But it would probably be good to act like he was into it. He pulled a twenty out of his pocket, folded it, and dropped it on the table in front of Mr. Pink. "On the seven horse in the tenth race."

Mr. Pink flicked the bill onto the floor. Anthony picked it up. What was the guy's deal? Was the waitress wrong about him?

"Are you still here?" Mr. Pink asked.

"Yeah, I heard . . ." Anthony's words trailed off as Mr. Pink's cool green eyes swept from the tips of Anthony's sneakers to the top of his head. *He's looking at me like I'm something he should be wiping off the bottom of his shoe,* Anthony thought. The hand not holding his beer automatically curled into a fist. And Mr. Pink gave a friggin' *chuckle.*

Anthony suddenly felt like a twelve-year-old trying to get into a pickup game of b-ball with some high school guys. But come on, who was this guy to be giving him attitude? He was just some lowlife bookie. Anthony reached down and snatched up his twenty. "Guess I heard wrong," he said.

"Yes, you did," Mr. Pink answered. He pulled the toothpick out of his martini and slid the olive off it with his teeth. He slowly chewed the olive, continuing to look at Anthony.

Anthony hesitated. All he wanted to do was slink away, especially now that all Mr. Pink's buds had started to watch the show. But he needed to ask about Aiden.

"Look, you want another drink?" Anthony blurted.

"No, I'm fine," Mr. Pink told him.

Does he know how much I would like to smash his superior face in? Anthony wondered. "I just . . . My aunt sent me here to look for my uncle and—"

He's not buying it, Anthony realized. "I'm looking for Aiden Matthews," he said, since all he could think to do was spit out the truth.

"He's not here," Mr. Pink said.

Big freaking news, Anthony thought. "Do you know where I can find him? I mean, you must know him. Since you know he's not here."

"He's not here," Mr. Pink repeated. It was clearly the end of the conversation.

Anthony turned around and started away from the table. What else could he do?

"Hey, kid," Mr. Pink called after him.

Anthony spun back to face Mr. Pink. He knew he looked way too excited, way too eager, but he couldn't help it.

"There's no tenth race today," Mr. Pink said.

"It says that school personnel and other relatives might be called in and asked questions during the psychiatric evaluation of a child or adolescent," Rae told Yana. She replaced the thick book back on the shelf.

"I'm so screwed," Yana answered. "My principal hates me. She acts like I'm some kind of rabid dog that should be put down."

Rae shook her head. "Remember that article we read on the MMPI-2. One of the things it tests for is exaggeration of problems. Too much exaggeration sends up a warning flag for the evaluator."

"Right," Yana answered. "What time does this place close, anyway?"

"We've got tons of time," Rae said. "The university library is always open late. So what do you want to read about next?"

"I'm still thinking about the part where they can ask my principal questions." Yana pulled another psychology textbook off the shelf but didn't open it. "How much do you think that means? Like, if my principal says I'm a bad seed or whatever, is that it? Do I get locked away?"

"My professional opinion would be no."

Rae swiveled her head toward the deep voice and saw a guy with sleek black hair grinning at her and Yana through an empty spot in the bookshelf.

"And we should take your professional opinion because?" Yana asked.

"Because I'm number two in my class. And number one is a complete weirdo who never leaves the library, which I think is a problem if you want to be a psychiatrist," the guy said. "I mean, she would always rather deal with a book than a person. Unlike me. I'm a people guy." He stuck his hand through the hole. "Lenny Kwan."

Rae shook his hand, careful not to let her fingertips

touch his. She didn't like to go fingertip-to-fingertip unless she absolutely had to. It was an invasion of privacy. And it always turned some part of her body numb. "Rae," she said to Lenny. "And that's Yana."

Yana shook his hand, too. "So my principal can't torpedo me?" she asked.

Lenny disappeared from the hole. "My friend's principal," he said as he walked around his aisle and into theirs. "That's how you're supposed to say it. *My friend's.* So that I won't think you're a freak."

"I don't care if you think I'm a freak," Yana told him.

Lenny laughed. "That's very healthy."

BUT YOU'RE NOT HEALTHY, RAE. YOU'RE SICK. VERY SICK. YOU SHOULD BE LOCKED AWAY RIGHT NOW. YOU DON'T BELONG OUTSIDE WITH THE REST OF US.

"What?" The word escaped from Rae's mouth in a squeak. Lenny and Yana both stared at her. "What . . . what else is important in a psychiatric evaluation, O genius people-guy?" Rae asked, trying to recover.

YOU CAN TRY AND ACT NORMAL. BUT IT DOESN'T WORK. I CAN SEE INSIDE YOU. IT'S SO EASY. IT'S SO CLEAR. THERE'S SOMETHING WRONG WITH YOU, RAE. AND IT'S GROWING. THAT'S MY PROFESSIONAL OPINION.

I'm not touching anything. Nothing, Rae told herself. *But those aren't my thoughts. Where are they coming from? What's happening to me now?* Her thoughts came as shrieks in her brain, so loud, so overpowering that she couldn't hear what Yana and Lenny were saying. They were talking to each other. She could see their lips moving. But she couldn't hear them at all.

What is happening to me? The shriek ripped into the soft gray matter of her brain.

RAE, RAE, RAE. YOU'RE GOING TO FALL TO PIECES RIGHT HERE, AREN'T YOU? LITTLE BLOODY PIECES TOO SMALL TO BE SAVED.

The not-her thought was quiet and calm. Nothing like Rae's frantic ravings. "I have to go to the bathroom," she announced. The words must have come out louder than she meant for them to because both Yana and Lenny looked startled.

"You want me to come with?" Yana asked.

"No, I'm fine. I'm fine," Rae answered. She rushed down the aisle and turned the corner. Her knees buckled, and it was all she could do to find an unoccupied row in the stacks. When she did, she sank down to the floor. She couldn't take another step.

Rae wrapped her arms around her legs and pressed her forehead to her knees, her eyes squeezed tightly shut. "Please let me be okay," she whispered. But she knew her prayer, if that's what it was, couldn't be answered. Because she wasn't okay. Something bad had already happened to her. Something very, very bad.

Anthony strode out of Jocks and Jills, yet another sports bar, and headed over to the Hyundai.

"Nothing?" Jesse asked when Anthony got in the driver's seat and slammed the door.

"Nothing," Anthony answered. "Guess you didn't see him going in or out?"

"Yeah, I did. That's why I'm sitting here like an idiot," Jesse shot back.

"Okay, dumb question," Anthony said. Jesse was in a bad mood because he wasn't old enough to get into a bar. Technically Anthony wasn't, either. But redheaded, freckle-faced Jesse looked even younger than he was. And when you were fourteen, that was rough. "There's still one more Jocks and Jills we can try."

"*You* can try, you mean," Jesse muttered.

Anthony ignored him. "And there are probably a bunch more bars that have a pretty much resident bookie. It's not only a sports-bar thing." He turned the ignition key and pulled out of the parking space.

"But that guy, Mr. Pink, he might be the only one Aiden deals with," Jesse answered, saying the thing that Anthony was trying not to let himself think.

"So what do you want to do, Jesse? Give up?" Anthony demanded. He swung out of the parking lot and immediately had to come to a stop for a red light.

"No, I'm just saying . . ." Jesse shook his head. "If you take Addison, we'll get there faster."

When the light changed, Anthony took the right onto Addison. He wasn't sure it would be faster—there was less traffic, but the speed limit was lower—but why not go with Jesse's suggestion, especially since he'd spent most of the day sitting in the car? "What's wrong with the guy behind us?" he complained. "He's trying to eat my bumper."

Jesse looked over his shoulder. "Anthony," he said, his voice suddenly urgent. "It's Aiden. His hair's different from the picture. But it's definitely him."

"What?" Anthony exclaimed.

Aiden pulled his car up alongside theirs, driving on the wrong side of the street, then he sped up, jerked his car in front of Anthony's, and skidded to a stop.

Anthony had to jam on the brakes, and he still tapped Aiden's car. "Wait here," he told Jesse. He jumped out of the Hyundai and hurled himself toward Aiden's car. "What in the hell are you doing?" he demanded as Aiden climbed out onto the street.

Aiden strode straight toward Anthony. "He's got a stun gun," Jesse shouted. Before Anthony could react, Aiden pressed the taser against Anthony's shoulder and set it off. Anthony went down hard.

Immediately he tried to stand back up. But it was like he'd forgotten how. He knew it involved moving his legs in a certain way. But how? How did you get your legs to move? How?

"Get away from him," Anthony heard Jesse shout.

Anthony wanted to order Jesse to stay in the car. But when he opened his mouth, a spasm went through his jaw. His lips twitched, and all he could get out was a grunting sound.

Aiden knelt down beside Anthony and rested his knee on Anthony's chest. "You get close, and I'll have to stun you, too," he warned Jesse. Then he lowered his head until his face was only inches away from Anthony's. "You're not going to be feeling too good for at least five minutes. The taser upset communication between your brain and body. So I want you to be good and lie there and think about whether you want me to shock you again or whether you want to tell me why you've been tracking me all over town."

Anthony managed to swallow. Then swallowed again. "Rae," he choked out. "Call them off Rae."

Aiden slid his knee off Anthony's chest. "Rae Voight? This is about Rae Voight?"

"Yeah, it's about Rae," Jesse burst out.

"What exactly happened?" Aiden demanded, his eyes never leaving Anthony's.

"Don't know . . . who for sure. But somebody's . . . trying . . . to scare her." Aiden helped Anthony sit up. A moment later he was able to continue. It was getting easier to make his lips and tongue do what he wanted them to do. "Somebody painted the word *unclean* on her locker," he got out. He coughed. "Tried to make it look like blood. We thought it could be the work of your goons."

Aiden's frown deepened. "Sounds like a prank. It's not the way an agent of the government works," he answered. He glanced at Jesse. "And by the way, they aren't my guys. Not anymore."

Anthony didn't care about Aiden's life story. "Who is it, then? Who's still after Rae?"

Aiden's eyes narrowed. "I don't know," he admitted.

Chapter 6

Rae and Lea Dessin hit the door to the locker room at the same time. Lea got this deer-in-the-headlights expression on her face, and Rae was afraid her face had gone all panicked Bambi, too. *We used to be best friends,* she thought. *How unbelievable is that?*

"So, um, what are you in this session?" Lea asked, holding the door open for Rae.

"Volleyball," Rae answered. "Can't you see the bruise on my forehead?" She lightly touched the tender spot.

"Don't you remember what I used to tell you? You're supposed to use your hands. Your *hands,*" Lea teased as she followed Rae inside.

"I know. But I hate that rule. I find it so much

easier to catch the ball with my head," Rae joked back. And they both laughed.

Weird. Does this little encounter mean that some-day Lea and I might actually be friends again? Rae wondered. It was kind of happening with Yana—the whole friendship repair. And Lea had never done anything to hurt Rae. Except, yeah, get freaked out whenever they were within two feet of each other. But she'd never intentionally gone after Rae the way Yana had. So maybe there was hope.

"See you later," Lea said, turning off at her locker row.

"See ya," Rae answered. Was that "see you later" real? Did Lea really hope she'd—

Enough, Rae told herself. She absolutely was not going to let herself get all gooey and hopeful over three words. Although at least the three words were real. They'd been said out loud by another person. They didn't just appear in Rae's head like the words had in the university library yesterday. Or the hospital the day before.

Rae turned down her own row. When she reached her locker, she grabbed the lock, a coat of wax protecting her fingers, and started to twist in the combination. The lock clattered to the floor. It had been cut open.

"No. No. This is not happening," Rae whispered.

She slowly swung open the door, her eyes shut. With a deep breath she forced her eyes back open, then winced when she saw what was waiting for her.

Red letters slashed across the metal. Rae blinked, trying to get the letters to come into focus.

Unclean blood. That's what the letters spelled out. What was that supposed to mean?

Maybe the words aren't even there, Rae thought. *Maybe it's just like the voices. Just a little . . .*

A little psychotic episode. Now, that's comforting. Rae gave her left hand a hard shake to get rid of the tremors racing through it, then reached out and ran her fingers over the letters. They were still the slightest bit wet, sticky, really, and when she pulled her hand away, the wax on her fingers had been stained red. Bloodred.

I don't know if I should be happy the letters are real or not, Rae thought as she got a whiff of the nail polish that had been used as paint. *It's not like it proves I'm sane, since there's still the voices thing. But it does prove that somebody is very interested in me.*

Just the government guys making sure I remember that I'm supposed to keep my head down and my mouth closed, Rae told herself. *That's all. No biggie. No biggie,* she repeated in her head, hating that she didn't feel totally convinced. Rae took a glance to the left and the right to make sure that none of the other girls had seen the message in her locker. It looked like they were all busy with getting out towels and hair dryers and makeup bags. Good. She definitely didn't want the love note in her locker to be the newest gossip item. She moved closer to the door, completely blocking the message with her body.

I won't bother with a shower, she decided. Volleyball the way she played it was not an aerobic activity. And if she hurried, she might get in a Marcus sighting before geometry. More than anything, that's what she needed right now.

She reached for the shell of her cashmere twinset, careful to use the hand with the unstained fingers. A sound that was half whine and half gasp escaped from her throat when she pulled the shell free. It was streaked with bright red blood.

No. Not blood. Calm down, she ordered herself. *It's nail polish. Only nail polish.* She checked her sweater and skirt. Those bastards. They'd splattered nail polish all over everything. Even her boots.

Rae threw the broken lock into her locker and slammed the door. She rushed out into the hall and immediately headed toward the principal's office. Not that she planned to try to sic the principal on the government people. Rae wasn't that deranged yet. But she needed a pass to get her out of the school and home, where she could get some fresh clothes. She was already getting some looks for walking around in her gym clothes outside the gym. But the looks were nothing compared to what she'd have gotten if she'd gone out in her hi-I'm-Carrie outfit.

Rae turned the corner, and two guys actually stopped walking and stared at her. Hadn't they ever seen a girl in gym clothes before? What, had they been living in a cave somewhere? She walked past them, ignoring the itchy feeling on her back that made her pretty sure they were still watching her. Losers.

When she reached the door to the principal's office, she took a moment to fluff her hair and straighten her T-shirt. Then she grabbed the door handle—and froze. Her eyes had locked on a bright red flyer posted on the bulletin board next to the door.

This is why people were staring at me, she realized, her stomach bunching up until she could feel her lunch knocking against the walls. *They read this. They know my secret, the secret I've been keeping, God, almost my whole life.*

She took a step closer to the bulletin board, her eyes locked on the words written on that flyer. It was all there—every disgusting detail. Melissa Voight, accused of killing her best friend, Erika Keaton. Found mentally incompetent to stand trial. Sent off to die in a mental institution. Crazy. Insane. A killer.

And Rae Voight's mother. It was right there, in clear print.

They think I'm the daughter of a lunatic murderer, Rae thought, her pulse racing. *Even though my mother didn't do anything like that, they think she did.*

Why wouldn't they? Everyone does. The lawyers. The judge. The reporter who wrote the article. Of course everyone at school is staring. I'm surprised they aren't running screaming at the sight of me. I mean, they already know I've had a breakdown. They're probably expecting me to grab an ax or an Uzi and go on a rampage any second.

She let go of the doorknob she'd still been clutching and ripped the flyer free. Another reminder from the government agency? Or could Anthony be right? Could someone else hate her enough to do this?

Maybe it's only been on the board for a few minutes, Rae thought. No one in gym had seen it. She would know if they had. She jammed the flyer into her pocket. *Maybe just three or four people saw it. Those two guys and the—*

Rae heard footsteps behind her and then soft, hissing whispers, whispers that she'd heard all the time after The Incident.

Maybe it's not about you, she thought. She forced herself to turn around. The two girls—sophomores she knew only by sight—suddenly sped up. But Rae had time to see that they each held a red flyer.

How many of these freakin' red flyers are there? Anthony thought as he walked through the hallways after school. He spotted one of the flyers taped to the trophy case, lunged toward it, ripped it down, and added it to the pile under his arm. "It'd be easier to torch the whole school," he muttered, snatching another flyer off the floor. And he'd be happy to light the match, especially if a couple of people who'd gotten their rocks off talking about Rae and her mom could somehow be trapped inside. Long enough to get a little singed, anyway.

Anthony pushed the image of the burning school out of his head. He needed to stay focused. Because, yeah, there was a red flyer sticking out of the backpack of the guy who'd just stepped away from the drinking fountain. Anthony picked up his pace and yanked the flyer out of the pack. "What in the hell are you doing?" the guy demanded. He spun around, and Anthony realized it was Chris McHugh from the football team.

"Why are you reading this crap?" Anthony demanded.

"It's interesting. What's your problem?" McHugh said.

"My problem is that Rae is—" What exactly was Rae to him? "She's Salkow's girlfriend, man," Anthony continued, because that was the only thing that he could think to tell McHugh. "Do you think Salkow really wants everybody in the place walking around with one of these?" He added McHugh's flyer to the pile.

"Yeah, well, maybe Salkow should think about if he did the right thing, getting back together with Rae," McHugh answered. "You weren't here last year. You didn't see her lose it. But I did. She was completely wacked. And now this comes out about her mom. What if it's one of those like-mother-like-daughter deals? Salkow could wake up some morning without his head."

All Anthony wanted to do was grab McHugh and mop the floor with him. It definitely wasn't one of those times where he'd be pissed off at himself afterward, either. He would bet any amount of money that thinking about having pulverized McHugh would end up one of his best memories. But every minute he spent dealing with McHugh was a minute he wouldn't be on red-flyer patrol. And getting rid of the flyers would do Rae a lot more good.

"Ignorant butt hole," he muttered as he walked past McHugh, allowing himself a hard shoulder knock on the way.

"What did you say?" McHugh called after him. Anthony didn't answer. He'd spotted a red flyer sticking halfway out of someone's locker. He tore it free and added it to his pile. Then he charged on. When he reached the corner, he swung left. His eyes zoomed immediately to Rae's locker. She was standing there. He knew she was almost as tall as he was, but she looked so small standing over there right now.

Anthony felt like a dozen fishhooks had just jabbed into his chest, going deep, digging into his heart. And then he was reeled in, reeled straight over to Rae. He was pretty sure she didn't want him over there, but he couldn't stop himself, not without doing some major damage to his body.

"Hi," he said. Because that's the kind of idiot he was, the kind who couldn't come up with anything better to say than "hi."

"Hi," Rae said back. But she didn't look him in the eye. She tried to make it seem like she was. But she was really focusing on his eyebrows.

This is bad. If she can't even look at me, she's a lot worse than I thought she'd be, Anthony thought. *I mean, crap, I already knew everything about her mom. And she knows I don't care. How could I care when my dad—*

Maybe you should actually attempt to spit out a few more words, Anthony interrupted himself. "Um, Rae, look, screw them all." He tore his stack of flyers in half.

Rae laughed. The sound made Anthony's stomach turn. There wasn't anything . . . anything *happy* about the laugh. It was like Rae was some freaky robot person from one of those movies about artificial intelligence. Like there was nothing real inside her. Nothing Rae.

"I mean it," Anthony insisted. "If they can't understand that what your mother did has nothing to do with you, forget them." He tore the flyers in half again. Rae still didn't meet his eyes. But at least she didn't let out another of those freaky laughs. "That's what you told me, at least basically, remember? When you found out that my dad killed someone in that armed robbery. You said it had noth—"

"She didn't even do it," Rae said softly. It was like she was talking to herself more than she was talking to him. "My dad gave me this letter from her, a letter she wrote before she died that was for me on my sixteenth birthday. She said she didn't kill Erika Keaton. And I touched every inch of the paper, and I didn't get one thought that told me she was lying."

Anthony blinked. "Are you serious?" he said, understanding just how huge this was for Rae. God, if he could find out that the deal with his dad killing someone was all some kind of crazy lie . . .

Not about you, Anthony reminded himself. "Rae, that's great," he said. "So then you really shouldn't care about this stupid stuff. You know the truth. Tell them all to go—"

"Rae," someone called. Anthony glanced over his shoulder and saw Marcus coming toward them. Maybe that was good. Anthony wanted to finish what he was saying to Rae, but it's not like it was getting through to her. Maybe Marcus could yank her out of the bad place.

"Get your stuff," Marcus told Rae. He gave Anthony a nod, barely seeming to care that he was there. "I'm taking you out for a pizza. With all the veggies it can hold, just the way you like it."

"Okay," she answered. "Okay, yeah, that would be good."

Anthony turned away and threw the ripped-up flyers into the trash. At least he'd done something for Rae. Not that she actually needed him to.

* * *

"Crowded," Marcus said.

"Yeah," Rae answered, even though the pizza place was only about half full. It was easier to agree. And God, what did it matter if half the tables were empty when most of the people who *were* in the place kept taking these sneaking, darting glances at Rae? She was pretty sure the group two tables away were hunched over a copy of the red flyer, getting every juicy, sordid detail about Rae's mother. What did she expect, coming to a place two blocks away from the school? But this was where Marcus had wanted to go, so . . .

She shot a look at Marcus. He was studying the menu, although they'd already ordered. And although he had to have the thing memorized. They'd come here a million times.

Marcus must have felt her watching him because he dropped the menu and smiled at her. "You look nice. I like that sweater." His forehead wrinkled a little. "Is that what you were wearing at lunch?"

He was such a guy. "No. I, uh, spilled something, and the principal let me run home and change," Rae answered. Why go into it? The whole nail-polish-spattered clothes incident seemed pretty minor now.

"Oh. Well, you look really nice." Marcus picked up the menu again.

"Are you thinking about dessert already?" Rae

asked, her voice coming out sounding a little too loud and a little too cheerful to her own ears. *Maybe that's 'cause you're putting on a show for everybody,* she thought. *The Look at How Rae Isn't at All Bothered by Having a Killer Mom Show.* That was the best she could do. It wasn't like she could tell Marcus or anyone else that she was sure her mother wasn't a killer because Rae's fingerprint-reading power had told her so. "You know you're going to have the monster cookie sundae, just like you always do," she went on, just as loud, just as cheerful, unable to stop the performance.

"Maybe this time I'll surprise you," Marcus answered, still reading the menu.

Didn't he have it memorized after all this time? she wondered again. Then it hit her. Like a punch to her gut. Marcus wasn't reading the menu. He was *hiding.*

And I did this to him, she thought. *I put him in a position where he has to hide from people who are his friends or who at least wish they were his friends.* Usually he was like a movie star in this place. He'd get asked for autographs if people weren't afraid of looking like losers.

"Be right back," Rae said. She didn't wait for an answer. She stood up and hurried over to the counter. "That pizza we ordered. We decided we want it to go," she told the girl behind the register. Two minutes later she was holding a hot pizza box in her hands. "Marcus," she called. When he looked over, she jerked her chin toward the door.

"What's going on?" he asked as he fell into step beside her.

"Why don't we go someplace more private?" She forced a smile. "I don't feel like sharing you right now." If she told him the truth—that she could tell it was torture for him to sit in the pizza place with her—then he'd insist she was wrong. And he'd insist that they stay to prove it.

"I never feel like sharing you," Marcus answered. He pulled open the door for her, then took the pizza and carried it to the car. "Where to?" he asked when he and Rae were both buckled into their seats.

"The park across from Lee Elementary," Rae answered. "We'll have a picnic." The little kids who hung out in the park wouldn't know anything about Rae's mother. So there'd be no stares, no stress.

"Great idea." Marcus grabbed Rae's hand and held it all the way over to the park. *Maybe we could live in the car. Keep on driving. That'd be nice,* she thought. But Marcus pulled into the parking lot next to the playground and let go of her hand.

"See that little donkey over there?" Rae asked after she climbed out of the car.

"That plastic thing's a donkey?" Marcus said.

"Of course it's a donkey. Look at the ears," Rae said. "Anyway, when I was little, I thought it was alive. I'd lie on the grass right here—" She sat down on the grass and patted the spot beside her. When Marcus joined her on the ground, she continued. "I'd lie here for hours, waiting for it to move. And sometimes . . . sometimes I thought it did."

Marcus raised one of his perfectly arched blond eyebrows. "Did you see it move?"

There was something off in the way he asked the question. *Oh God. He's thinking it was some early sign of insanity, the insanity I got from my mother.*

She wished she could tell him the truth. But to explain that her mother hadn't been crazy, she'd have to explain that her mother had been given a battery of treatments to enhance her psychic ability. She'd have to explain that the scientist who gave her the treatments decided she was dangerous and made sure she died in the mental hospital.

And if Rae tried to explain even a little of that, Marcus would be absolutely certain that Rae was nuts. Who could blame him?

Rae realized Marcus was still staring at her. "You know how little kids are. I was at the age where I still believed in Santa and the Easter bunny," she said quickly, then opened the pizza box and handed Marcus a slice.

She'd planned to try and make their picnic totally fun and light. But maybe that wasn't the way to go. Rae couldn't tell Marcus the truth. She couldn't even try to explain why she felt so sure that her mother had never killed anyone. Explaining that would mean explaining Rae's fingerprint-reading ability. Still, that didn't mean there was nothing Rae could say to Marcus. There was a little bit of truth she could tell. "You—I guess you're probably wondering why I never told you about my mother," Rae said. "I mean, about the murder and the—the mental hospital."

Marcus took a huge bite of his pizza, then shook his head. "No," he mumbled. He chewed in silence for a moment, then swallowed hard. "No," he repeated more clearly. "It makes sense you wouldn't want to talk about it. *I* wouldn't have wanted to talk about it."

"Even to me?" Rae protested.

"Even to you. So don't worry about it," Marcus said. "Hey, look at that kid," he said, pointing. "He's done skin the cat four times in a row, and he's going for five."

Okay, so he doesn't want to talk about it, Rae thought. *That's fine. That's good. We can just keep*

everything between us the way it was. We won't let
any of this outside garbage touch us.

Anthony scanned the bowling alley, and his
heart slowed down a little when he saw Aiden
Matthews waiting for him by lane eight, just the
way he'd agreed to. Anthony had been afraid he'd
have to track Aiden down again. And he would
have done it. But he was glad he didn't have to.
He didn't want to have to waste any time. He
wanted to figure out exactly who was harassing
Rae—with full names, addresses, and phone num-
bers included.

"Here's the flyer I told you about. They were all
over the school." He thrust a flyer into Aiden's hands
and plopped down in one of the molded plastic
chairs.

"Uh-huh, uh-huh," Aiden muttered as he read. He
sat down next to Anthony. "I still say this isn't the
work of anyone in the agency. If I were you, I'd look
for someone—"

"Hold it. What's this 'if I were you' bull?" Anthony
demanded. "You're in this until the end. You owe
Rae that. That and a hell of a lot more."

"I gave you my cell phone number because I care
about what happens to Rae, and I wanted to do what
I could to help," Aiden responded calmly. "But at

this point having any contact with me could put Rae in more danger."

"That's more bull," Anthony interrupted again. "You're not worried about Rae. You're worried about yourself."

Aiden gave a tug on his graying ponytail, then he sighed. "Maybe you're right. At least partly. As you know, I *was* forced to clear out of my own house." He frowned. "But the truth is that if Rae is seen near me, the agency could very well decide to come after us both."

"So you'll stay away from her. You'll go through me," Anthony said. As far as he was concerned, Rae never had to know that Anthony was in contact with Aiden. "Listen, on the phone before, you were starting to say something about Erika Keaton."

"Right. I was saying that the fact that the flyers make reference to Erika Keaton's murder makes it even more definite that this has nothing to do with the agency, for several reasons."

Anthony waited, and finally Aiden continued.

"First, the agency knows—well, we are all quite confident that Rae's mother didn't actually kill Erika."

Anthony's eyes narrowed. "That's what Rae said."

The muscles in Aiden's neck tightened. "What does Rae know? What exactly?"

Anthony frowned. "She doesn't know anything," he said carefully. He wasn't about to mention the letter or Rae's fingerprint power. Yeah, Aiden probably knew all about what Rae could do, but Anthony wasn't going to be the one to spill it—just in case. Who knew how much he could trust this guy? "It's just that she's sure her mom didn't kill anyone," Anthony continued. "But what makes you guys think that?"

Aiden looked away. "I feel certain—as do most of the members of the agency—that that kind of violent action didn't fit Rae's mother's personality profile."

"Even with the experiments you guys did on her?" Anthony pressed.

"The experiments didn't change the basic character of the person involved," Aiden answered.

"So what's your theory? Who do you believe killed Erika?" Anthony asked.

Aiden picked up a pencil and began doodling on one of the bowling score pads. "I—we—don't know. We just never accepted the police's version. We never believed Melissa Voight was capable of murder."

He's holding something back, Anthony thought. *There's no way some government agency just thinks that Rae's mom was too* nice *to kill someone. He's got to know more.* Anthony decided not to pressure him. For now. There was too much else he needed to know first.

"So what's your theory on who put those flyers all over school?" he asked, over the crashing sound of someone getting a strike in the next lane.

"As I said, I'm sure it wasn't anyone from the agency," Aiden said. "Aside from their feelings about Melissa actually committing the murder, they wouldn't want people talking about the incident." Aiden started doodling faster. "Just on the off chance that someone got interested in the group that Erika and Melissa were both members of."

"We've covered who you think it isn't," Anthony said. "Now who do you think it *is*?"

Aiden tilted his head to the side. "To be honest, the personal nature of these attacks makes it seem like someone is trying to avenge Erika Keaton's death. Since Melissa is dead, they seem to have moved on to Rae."

"So we have to find whoever it is. And fast." Anthony stood up and paced around the table with the plastic score sheet in the center. "Does Erika have any relatives around here or anything?"

"Not that I know of. She was an only child, she didn't have any children, and her parents are dead." Aiden paused. "But there could be some relatives out there. I'll do some checking. I still have some sources."

"And what should I do?" Anthony asked. He had to do something. Anything.

"Wait until you hear from me," Aiden replied.

Wait. Aiden said that like it was easy. What if Anthony was waiting for Rae to get killed?

Chapter 7

So what could top Rae's mom's being a murderer in Sanderson Prep's gossip? Rae asked herself as she walked to the cafeteria the next day. She needed something to keep her thoughts off all the stares and whispers that were following her everywhere. Hmmm. Maybe if someone's dad was a cross-dresser. That might do it. *There would need to be visual aids, though,* she decided. Like if someone did a purple flyer that showed Vince's dad in a satin bra and panty set, that could become the day's hot topic. Especially because the murder Rae's mom supposedly committed happened before any of the people at school were even in kindergarten.

Maybe I could do some kind of fake photo, Rae

thought. *I could take J Lo's body in some outrageous outfit and put—*

But no, she wasn't that sadistic. And anyway, no matter what new gossip came up, no one was going to forget that Rae was the possibly insane child of an insane slash homicidal mother. They might latch onto a new juicy tidbit about somebody else, but that didn't mean they'd ever forget about Rae. Well, screw them if they couldn't deal. She was who she was.

"Hey, you." Rae glanced over her shoulder and saw Marcus heading up to her. "Turn around. We're not doing the caf today. I'm taking you to this new place I heard about over in Little Five Points."

Rae turned to face him. "Kind of far away, isn't it? Will we be able to eat and make it back in time?"

Marcus took her by the shoulders and started walking backward down the hall, pulling her with him. "We'll get it to go and eat in the car on the way back. Come on. It's supposed to be amazing. With falafel and hummus and all that stuff you like."

"You hate that stuff," Rae reminded him as he maneuvered her toward the exit.

"But you like it. And I like you," Marcus answered. "So pick up the pace or we'll be late for fourth period."

Rae could barely keep up with him. He was

practically dragging her along with him, as if the school was on fire.

It's not just the pizza place I ruined for him, Rae realized. *It's the caf, too.*

Wait. No. *Nothing's ruined if we don't let it be,* she thought. *Forget them if they can't deal. That's your new philosophy, remember?*

Rae stopped short, refusing to budge even though Marcus kept tugging at her. "You know what? If we keep hiding, it'll make people stare more. We should just stop slinking around, eat here, let everyone say what they're gonna say and—"

"What are you talking about?" Marcus protested. He ran his hands down her arms. "I just wanted to do something nice for you. I thought, you know, since the last couple of days haven't been so great." His eyes darted around the hall, making it painfully obvious that his real concern was for them not to be spotted.

But he actually believes it. He actually thinks he's doing me some big favor, Rae thought. *When he wants to get away from the stares more than I do.*

"Why haven't we talked about it—about my mom?" she asked suddenly. "It's actually pretty stupid of us to pretend nothing's happened. It's not like it really makes it go away."

"Rae, come on. We're blocking traffic," Marcus

said. He gave her wrists a pull. "Let's just go try the place."

Out of the corner of her eye Rae caught sight of Lea walking by them, pretending not to see them. Clearly she didn't feel like being seen around Rae. And Marcus felt the same way. He was just being less obvious about it. And trying to make himself believe that wasn't even what was going on with him.

Rae yanked free of Marcus's grasp. She walked over to the little marble bench next to the drinking fountain and sat down. She needed to think, think hard, and she couldn't do that with Marcus yanking on her.

"What?" Marcus strode up and stood in front of her. "What, Rae?" he asked impatiently.

"Nothing," Rae answered. "Nothing," she repeated. Why shouldn't Marcus want to avoid the stares and whispers? It wasn't like he didn't want to be with her. He just didn't want to be with her *here*. "Let's just go."

Anthony pulled up in front of Jesse's house and honked. A second later Jesse burst through the door, sprinted to the car, and got in. "What's up? Did something happen? All my mom said was that you called and you were coming over because you wanted to go get ice cream."

"Aiden found a storage space Mercer was renting," Anthony explained, wondering where Jesse got that endless energy. "It's crammed with stuff. But Aiden thinks maybe something in there could lead us to whoever's still after Rae."

"What about the government people? They didn't clear it out?" Jesse asked.

Man, he's quick, even with all that nonstop babbling, Anthony thought as he drove down the street. *Jesse's the one who should be at Sanderson Prep, not me.*

"Aiden was the point guy on the Steve Mercer situation," he replied. "He was getting close to finding the storage facility when he decided to quit. He's the only one who knows where it is."

"He quit?" Jesse popped the glove box and slammed it shut a couple of times. "I didn't think you could just quit if you were part of a secret government organization." He shrugged. "At least you can't on TV."

"He told me he quit. But who knows. He made it hard enough to find him the other day," Anthony answered. He made a left at the corner, glanced at the little map he'd drawn for himself, and got in the right lane.

"And if he quit and it was all fine with everybody, he probably wouldn't have moved out of his place so fast," Jesse said.

"Yeah. But you know what? I don't really care

either way. All I want is whatever info Aiden can get us." Anthony made the right turn. "Look for a sign that says Lock, Stock, and Barrel. It should be on the left in the next couple of blocks."

"Right there," Jesse said, pointing to a sign that was so faded, Anthony might have missed it.

"Got it." Anthony made the left and found a spot in the parking lot of the storage place. It wasn't hard. The lot had only two other cars. "Doing big business here," he muttered as he climbed out of the Hyundai. "Aiden said we're supposed to meet him at storage shed number nine," he told Jesse.

In silence they walked across the parking lot, through the sagging gate of the chain-link fence, and down the first row of sheds. "Wonder if Mercer was broke or if he thought nobody would ever come looking for anything in this dump," Jesse finally said. His voice sounded twice as loud as normal in the deserted alley between the sheds.

"Maybe both," Anthony answered. "The layout makes no sense. We just passed number eight, and now this one says thirteen."

"It's over here," a voice called. Anthony turned toward the sound and saw Aiden standing in the half-open doorway of a shed off to the right. "I'm glad you brought help," he told Anthony as Anthony and Jesse headed up to him. "It's—well, see for yourself." He stepped back, and Anthony ducked inside the shed.

"It's worse than my room," Jesse joked as he squeezed into the shed.

"I haven't gotten too far," Aiden explained. He wiped the sweat off his forehead with the sleeve of his shirt and left a trail of dirt behind. "Just through those five boxes in the corner."

So that was five down and who the hell knew how many 'o go, Anthony thought. The place was only about as big as a one-car garage, but the boxes went from floor to ceiling, with only a couple of tiny paths running between the stacks.

"Is it okay to drag a box outside?" Jesse asked.

Aiden's mouth formed a thin line. "Better not," he answered. "I don't think anyone else knows about this place. But better not. So pick a box, any box."

"What should we be looking for, exactly?" Jesse asked.

"Could be lots of different things," Aiden answered. "Definitely anything about Rae or her mother. And anything about Erika Keaton and her relatives. I managed to track down a couple of her cousins. They live out of state and haven't been to Atlanta in years. That's what I got from local sources. But we might get info on other relatives from Mercer's files."

"I still don't get this whole Erika Keaton relative thing," Jesse said as he ripped open a box. "It doesn't make sense. Even if they blame Rae's mom, it's not like Rae did anything."

"People do stupid things for stupid reasons all the time," Aiden answered. He nodded in the direction of the other side of the room. "Like I said, I've been stacking the boxes I've gone through over in that corner. Put yours over there when you're done."

"Sounds good," Anthony said. He wrestled a box down into one of the clear paths and used his pocketknife to slice through the thick bands of packing tape. His gut clenched when he opened the box and saw that it was full of notebooks. His reading had gotten better. A lot better. But it would take him a lifetime to get through even just the notebooks in this box.

Then you'd better get started, right? he asked himself. He snatched up the top notebook and flipped it open. *I'm not going to be able to do this. I'm too freaking stupid,* he thought. He shoved the notebook back in the box, grabbed another one, and flipped through the pages.

"Aiden," he called. "I—" He hesitated. *Just say it,* he ordered himself. "I'm not going to be able to handle this box. All the notebooks in it have, I don't know, chemical formulas or something."

"We should start another stack for Mercer's lab notes," Aiden answered. "I'll have to think about whether there's anybody we can trust to help us interpret them."

Anthony dove into the task of clearing a space in another corner for the boxes of science stuff. This he could do. Picking up heavy stuff. That's what he was good for. When he'd moved everything there was to move, he opened another box. More science garbage. He hoisted the box over his head and maneuvered it into place in the science stack. Then he pulled out his pocketknife and started to attack another box.

"You guys have to see this," Jesse called out, his voice getting higher with every word.

He sounds freaked, Anthony thought as he shoved his way through the boxes and over to Jesse's side. "What?"

"It seems like everything in this box is about Rae. Check this out." Jesse thrust a folder into his hands. Anthony flipped it open and saw a photo of Rae. She looked nervous, hyperalert, like she'd heard someone following her. And she had. The bastard taking the picture.

Anthony flipped through the folder. All it had in it was photos of Rae. Rae painting in the empty art room. Had to have been taken with a telephoto lens. Rae walking through Little Five Points with Yana, carrying a shopping bag and laughing. Rae in the car with her dad. Rae coming out of Oakvale, looking wiped out, probably after an especially nasty group therapy session. Rae and Anthony standing in Rae's driveway, hugging. As he looked at the photo, he could almost feel her body pressed up against his, almost feel her hair against his cheek. That night had been one of the worst ones of his life, and Rae had been there for him. She'd—

Not the time for thinking about that, Anthony told himself. He handed the folder off to Aiden, who'd managed to squeeze in between him and Jesse.

Anthony reached into the box and pulled out a notebook. Mercer had sure loved his notebooks. He opened it and focused his attention the way he needed to when he read.

Rae Voight is exhibiting signs, Anthony read slowly, mouthing the words. *It is time for me to take action. If she lives, there is no way to tell what she will do with her powers. I must eliminate her. I must eliminate the risk. It is the only logical choice. More than that, it is my responsibility. When I look at Rae, I see the greatest mistake of my life. Killing her is the only way of redeeming myself.*

Anthony's hands started to shake so hard that he had to put the notebook down. *Mercer's dead,* he reminded himself. *He can't hurt Rae. He's dead.*

But somebody was still after Rae. And Anthony had no idea who it was. Or where they were. Or what they would do next.

He dug into the box and pulled out another note-book. He needed answers. Fast.

"Okay, you're up, Rae," Ms. Abramson said.

I wish Jesse were here, Rae thought. She liked talking mostly to him when she had to do her how-I'm-doing recap in group therapy. It was just good to have a friendly face to look at when you spewed. And she could really use a friendly face today, when any second she could start hearing voices in her head. Not a happy circumstance when you were busy trying to demonstrate your sanity.

Not that Ms. Abramson didn't have a friendly face. But she was always so intense, so focused on every word, that it ended up making Rae nervous. Ms. Abramson always seemed to see so much, like she was able to peer into the inside of your mind. Was Rae going to be able to convince her that all was right in Rae-world?

I guess I should say basically what I said to Abramson on the phone, Rae thought. *Do the I'm-so-happy speech. Yeah, it's all a big fat lie. But there's no way I'm going to start babbling about the voices in my head. Even I know that that's textbook schizophrenia.*

"Things are great, actually," Rae began. "I have to give you all a dork alert before I say this, but I got to be Moonbeam Queen at this dance at my school, which is kind of a big deal. And it made me feel *normal* again, you know?"

Rae glanced around the room and saw a couple of girls giving her nods. But Ms. Abramson wasn't. She was looking at Rae like she wasn't buying a word Rae was saying. *Can she see it?* Rae wondered. *Can she see the craziness that I keep shoving down?*

"Go on," Ms. Abramson urged.

"Um, okay. My boyfriend and I danced almost every dance. And—" She struggled to come up with something else to say. "And I'm doing volleyball in PE. I caught a ball with my head, but other than that, school's fine." *Other than that and a few flyers about my mom being a psycho killer, emphasis on the psycho,* she added silently.

Ms. Abramson seemed to be waiting for Rae to say more. *Probably she wants me to cough up something a little negative,* Rae thought. *What's therapy without a painful revelation or two?*

"My boyfriend, it's great between us," Rae said in a rush. "But sometimes, when he looks at me, I think he's remembering last spring. I mean, he was there when I had the breakdown. I don't think he's ever been able to get it out of his head. It's like . . . it's like sometimes he's waiting for it to happen again."

"Could you be projecting?" Riley Simpson asked, shooting a little glance at Ms. Abramson to see if she approved of his insightful question. Riley'd only been in the group a few weeks, and he was still in full-out butt-kissing mode. "It sounds like you might really be afraid that you're going to have another breakdown, but you've decided to tell yourself that it's your boyfriend who has those fears."

"That's an interesting observation, Riley," Ms. Abramson said. "What do you think, Rae? Are you experiencing any doubts about your mental health? It would be completely natural if you were."

Oh my God. Kill me now, Rae thought. *Or better yet, kill Riley.* Yeah, she was afraid she might be heading for another breakdown. Voices in your head were never a good sign. But she absolutely wasn't projecting anything onto Marcus.

"I guess sometimes I still worry," Rae answered. "But not as much as I used to." She'd wanted to throw Ms. Abramson a bone, and she had. But that was it.

"We'll all be interested to hear how you're doing with those fears at our next session," Ms. Abramson told her. "We're out of time for today."

The horrible sound of metal chair legs squeaking against the floor filled the room as everyone charged for the door. Rae led the pack. When she made it out of the main exit, it was like her entire body let out a sigh of relief.

Until she remembered what she had to do next. She was supposed to meet up with Yana at the hospital to see how Yana's psychiatric evaluation had gone. Just the thought of going into that place again made all of Rae's muscles go tight as guitar strings. Tighter. So tight, it felt like the slightest wrong move could snap them all, leaving Rae in a motionless heap.

Suck it up, Rae told herself as she headed to the bus stop. *You've got to do whatever you can to make sure Yana doesn't end up in the hospital.* Friend, not friend—it didn't matter. If a total stranger needed help staying out of a straitjacket, Rae'd probably do it.

She spotted the bus coming down the street and jogged the last few steps to the stop. The doors wheezed open, and Rae climbed on. In about half an hour she'd be at the hospital.

Rae spent the half hour figuring out exactly

how tight the muscles in her body could get. By the time she entered the hospital, her neck muscles felt like they'd hardened into granite. Like if she wanted to turn her head, she'd have to grab it with both hands and yank. Except her arm muscles might do the snapping thing if she tried to lift her arms that high.

"You're finally here." Rae wrenched her head toward the voice and saw Yana rushing toward her.

"How'd it go?" she asked. Her vocal cords were so taut that it hurt to speak. *Calm down,* she ordered herself. *I know you hate this place, but you'll be out in less than an hour.*

What if that's all it takes? Rae thought. *What if in less than an hour somebody here, a doctor, a nurse, figures out that I've been hearing voices? Then I might never, ever get out.*

"I aced it," Yana answered. "At least I'm pretty sure I did. The info I got from the guy at the library really helped." She moved closer to Rae and lowered her voice. "But I want you to make sure for me. Do that thing where you touch fingertips with Dr. Hachin."

"Okay," Rae agreed. That's what she was here for. To help Yana. "How do we get to her?"

"Not a problem. I told Hachin that you were meeting me and that we wanted to visit Lori Douglass.

She put us on the visitors list. It'll be easy to 'run into' Hachin on the ward," Yana told her.

"Lori Douglass is still in here?" Rae asked as she followed Yana over to the reception desk. Yana waited to answer until she'd told the nurse who they wanted to see and they'd both signed in.

"She was out for a little while, I think," Yana said as they made their way over to the elevators. "But you know the stats. Not everyone can make it on the outside."

God, please don't let me be one of those, Rae thought. *You haven't heard the voices all day,* she reminded herself. *You're doing good. Don't panic.* The middle elevator opened with a ding, and Rae managed to get the screaming muscles in her legs to work well enough to bring her inside. She used the short ride to rub the wax off her fingertips.

"Lori's in 414," Yana said when the elevator doors opened. She led the way down the hall. Like it was no big deal. When they reached 414, Yana gave a tap on the door and went in without waiting for an answer.

Rae remembered that. How there was no privacy in the hospital. Nurses would even come into the room in the middle of the night and check on you while you slept. Reluctantly she entered Lori's room without being invited.

Lori didn't even look at Rae and Yana at first. She

kept on watching a rerun of *Sabrina*. Rae was glad. It gave her time to get a decent expression on her face. It was so hard to slap on a smile when Lori looked . . . she looked disgusting. Like something out of a horror movie. Her hair had gotten really thin—she was almost bald in some places. And her body was almost all bones. *She's stopped eating again,* Rae thought. *They had to put her on intravenous.* Rae tried not to look at the needle going into Lori's stick-thin, bruised-up arm.

A commercial came on, and Lori turned her head toward Rae. Her eyes locked on Rae's face.

YOU CAN HAVE THE BED NEXT TO MINE, RAE. YOU NEED IT. I CAN TELL. PRETTY SOON EVERYONE WILL BE ABLE TO TELL. WHY DON'T YOU JUST LIE DOWN RIGHT NOW? LET THE DOCTORS TAKE CARE OF YOU. THAT'S WHAT YOU NEED.

"No," Rae burst out. She could almost feel a needle in her own arm. She could almost smell the bleach on the hospital sheets, feel the firm pillow under her head.

"No what?" Yana asked. Lori didn't say anything. She seemed pretty zonked. Who knew if she even recognized Rae or Yana?

"I didn't mean to say that out loud," Rae whispered. "It's just that Lori looks worse than I thought."

"Dr. Hachin!" Yana exclaimed. She rushed to the door and pulled it open. "Hey. You said you'd like to say hello to Rae, and here she is."

Do this one thing and you're out of here, Rae told herself, her head starting to feel like someone had been hitting it with a hammer. *You can do it. Just hang on until you get outside and you can freak out as much as you need to.*

Dr. Hachin stepped into the room. Rae decided not to waste any time. "It's good to see you," she said. She reached out her hand, and Dr. Hachin took it, then Rae let her fingertips slide down until they were directly over the doctor's.

As always, the rush of information almost overwhelmed her. Pieces of memories, fantasies, and dreams flew from Dr. Hachin into Rae. Rae's feet got the sensation of wearing the first pair of high heels Dr. Hachin had ever known. Her fingers got the sensation of playing a piano, the keys smooth and cool. Her cheek got the sensation of being slapped, slapped so hard, her cheekbone felt like it shattered.

She got fragments of thoughts, too. Worries about Lori's treatment. Realization that she'd skipped a car payment. So many thoughts, it was hard to track them. *Where's Yana in here? I need to get info about Yana before we break contact. Yana, Yana, Yana.*

Clean and clear as black LaserJet letters printed on smooth white paper, Rae got what she needed. But not what she'd hoped for.

Have to arrange a room for Yana and decide on a treatment program.

Rae slid her hand away from Dr. Hachin's and stared at her. She was really going to do it. She was going to have Yana committed.

Chapter 8

"**H**urry up, okay?" Yana urged. "He'll be home soon."

Rae nodded, then she reached out and ran her fingers over the can of shaving cream in Yana's dad's bathroom. At first the piercing pain of her headache was all she could focus on. Then the not-Rae thoughts shoved their way through.

/Jeanette doesn't want/with Yana gone/freakin' three percent raise/Yana screwing up every/Jeanette says/

Again Rae felt anger take over her body. But this time it was cold anger, not the hot, impulsive anger she'd felt the last time. As the thoughts rushed through her, they turned her subhuman. Calculating. Willing to do whatever she had to do. Ruthless.

Rae shivered. What must it be like to have a

father who was so dead inside? *That's not the most important question now,* she told herself. She didn't want to go back into the mind of Yana's dad, but she forced herself to reach out and do a fingerprint sweep of the handle of his toothbrush.

/hospital will cost/need her gone/loose filling/got to come up with the money/Jeanette's fed up/Yana's more trouble than/

Yana pulled the toothbrush out of Rae's hand. "I heard his car in the driveway. Come on. He'll freak out if he finds us in here. His bathroom is off-limits."

"Do you think there's a couple of aspirin in here I could steal?" Rae asked.

"Sure. Whatever." Yana jerked open the medicine cabinet, grabbed a bottle of aspirin and shook a few into her palm, then handed them to Rae. Rae dry-swallowed them as she followed Yana into Yana's bedroom, the aspirin leaving a streak of bitterness all the way from the back of her tongue to the base of her throat.

"Well?" Yana asked when she'd closed the door behind them. Rae sat down on the edge of Yana's perfectly made bed and rubbed her temples. It felt like her brain was trying to shove its way out of her skull. She'd never had a headache this bad. The numb spot she'd gotten from going fingertip-to-fingertip with Dr. Hachin was in her left big toe. *So* not helpful. "Well?" Yana said again.

"Sorry. Headache," Rae answered. She let out a sigh. "It seems like Jeanette is a big part of the deal. Like your dad—"

"Wants me out of the way so he can spend all his time with her," Yana finished. She flopped down on the bed next to Rae, and the motion sent a spike of pain into Rae's head.

"Something like that," Rae answered. "I didn't really get specifics. Just that your dad wanting you, uh, you know, out of the house was all mixed in with thoughts about Jeanette."

"So I guess my only hope is convincing him that I like Jeanette, and that I'm happy for them, and that I love her being around so much, and blah, blah, blah," Yana said.

"I think it's your best shot," Rae agreed.

"I should do it now. Who knows when the padded wagon will be pulling into the driveway with my straitjacket." Yana pushed herself to her feet. "Will you stay until I'm done talking to him?" she asked.

"Of course," Rae answered. All she wanted to do was go home, crawl into bed, and stay there until her headache went away. But she couldn't leave Yana now. If Yana couldn't convince her dad to stop the commitment process . . .

Rae wouldn't even allow herself to think about what would happen. "Good luck," she told Yana.

"I'm going to need it," Yana answered.

Rae thought Yana was right, that she was going to need all the luck there was. But she didn't say so. She just smiled an encouraging smile as Yana headed out the door. Then she lay back, closed her eyes, and let her world become the pounding of her headache.

Gradually the pounding became more of a tapping. Rae checked the alarm clock by Yana's bed. *She's been out there for almost an hour,* Rae realized. She strained her ears, trying to hear something that would let her know how it was going. But she didn't get even a snippet of a word. *At least they aren't in a yelling match,* she thought.

Rae rolled over on her side and reached for the phone. She could use a little dose of Marcus right now. What a hellish day it had been. Especially hearing those voices in her head in the hospital. God.

Hearing Marcus's voice will make me forget all about those other ones, she thought as she punched in his number. A smile broke across her face when he picked up and said hello. One word and she was smiling.

"Hey, it's me. What's up?" Rae said.

"Nothing much," Marcus answered.

"I'm hanging out with a friend right now. But I was thinking maybe I could come over after. Watch some forbidden TV," Rae said. *Translation: snuggle*

up with you, get all cozy with your arms around me,
and ignore the TV completely.

"Uh, I don't . . . My parents are having people over for dinner tonight, so . . ."

"You want to escape? Meet up at my place?" Rae wasn't going to try and get him out in public right now. It obviously made him hugely uncomfortable. She still thought it would be better to let everyone get a nice, long look, get it over with. But she'd play it his way if it made him happy.

"There's not really that much to do at your place," Marcus answered.

Not much to do? Like he needed something more than *her*?

Rae swallowed. She was trying so hard to believe that they could get through this. That it wouldn't be like last time.

"So let's go somewhere, then," Rae suggested. "Someplace nobody at school would be caught dead in. Like the roller rink! Wouldn't that be funny? We could skate to all the couples-only songs and watch all the little junior high kids in love." There was a long pause. "Marcus? You still there?"

"Yeah," Marcus answered. "And the skating thing would be fun. It's just . . . well, the thing is, Trish Ballard is having this party tonight, and I should probably put in an appearance. She's head cheerleader, you know. And all the guys on the team are pretty much expected to show."

"Right," Rae said, tears jumping to her eyes faster than she would have thought possible. "And you don't want me with you." She grabbed one of Yana's pillows and squeezed it tight against her chest.

"It's not that," he argued. "It's just that I—I didn't think it would be fun for you. Everybody'd be talking about your mom."

"Stop doing that!" Rae cried. "Stop acting like you're doing *me* a favor when you're really being a wuss."

"What are you talking about?" Marcus exclaimed.

Rae hurled the pillow across the room. "I'm talking about the fact that I'd have no problem with going to that party. I don't give a rat's butt what people say. I'd have fun because I'd be with you. You're the one with the problem, Marcus."

"I was trying to be considerate, and you—" Marcus began.

Rae interrupted him. "Bull. If you were trying to be considerate, you would have invited me to the party and helped me deal with everyone. Not have left my side for a second. And if you couldn't deal with that and you still wanted to be *considerate,* you'd have come over to my place—where no one would have seen you—and hung out with me. But you—"

"Rae—"

"You don't get to talk right now," Rae cut him off. "It's happening again. I can't believe I didn't realize it. But it's happening all over again. This is exactly like when I went into the hospital. You couldn't handle that, either, remember? You didn't break up with me or anything. You just never came to visit. And oh, yeah, you hooked up with Dori Hernandez."

"You're getting all worked up over nothing," Marcus told her. "I'm not hooking up with anyone. I'm just going to the party for a few—"

"Go to as many parties as you want. With whoever you want. Get yourself a whole entourage of Doris. Doesn't matter to me," Rae told him. "We're over. Forever." She hung up the phone before he could come up with some pathetic thing to say.

Anthony ripped open another box, not bothering to use his pocketknife. More science bull on top. He dug through the papers with both hands. Science, science, science. Another whole box full of science. That wasn't going to help Rae.

Aiden flipped through the pages of the notebook he was holding. "I've got something," he announced, a tremor running through his voice. "This is crazy," he murmured, more to himself than to Anthony and Jesse.

Anthony was on his feet instantly, heading over to Aiden. "What is it?" he demanded.

"Well, as we know, Mercer was tracking the offspring of everyone in the group," Aiden said, his eyes never leaving the notebook. "And of course, so were we. We never had any information about Erika Keaton having a child. But—according to these notes, it seems Mercer was convinced that Erika did give birth." He shook his head. "Fascinating."

"What does it say?" Anthony asked, the frustration nearly ripping him apart.

Aiden cleared his throat. "It says that Erika left town in the middle months of her pregnancy and returned after the baby was born, leaving the baby to be raised by someone else. He didn't know who." Aiden turned a few more pages. "This whole notebook is devoted to theories about where the child might be now."

"So this kid, he could be the one going after Rae," Anthony burst out.

"The agency had no suspicions of a Keaton offspring," Aiden insisted. "I wonder if Mercer was right or if he'd become delusional to the point—"

"We're checking it out," Anthony interrupted. "It doesn't matter if there's a ninety-nine percent chance Mercer was wacked—we're checking it out."

"You said he was tracking all the offspring," Jesse piped up. "Does that mean Mandy Reese, too?"

"We're not here to find out about Mandy Reese. No one is after Mandy Reese," Anthony said. He grabbed the box of science junk, lifted it over his head, and hurled it toward the pile of other boxes of science junk. It didn't get that close, and he couldn't care less.

"But Steve Mercer killed Mandy's mom, just like he killed Rae's mom," Jesse pushed.

"I know that," Anthony answered. "But Mercer's dead. So it can't be him who's after Rae. We have to forget about him for now. Forget about Mandy, too. She has no reason to want revenge on Rae, so we're not interested in her."

"I met her, okay?" Jesse shot back. "I just don't want anything to happen to her."

"I think Anthony's right," Aiden said. "We're almost positive there's a connection between the fact that Rae's mother was accused of killing Erika Keaton and the threats Rae's been getting. This should have nothing to do with Mandy." He used the bottom of his T-shirt to wipe off his sweaty face. *He's in decent shape for an old guy,* Anthony thought. That was good. If they needed to get physical when they finally found out who was after Rae, then—

Mr. Potato Head, the guy who's after Rae isn't going to start throwing punches if you find him, Anthony told himself. *He's probably going to start shooting. And being in shape—not gonna help.*

"We need to find out more about Keaton's kid," Anthony said. He opened another box. They weren't even halfway through. And maybe that was good. Because they hadn't found one thing—one *useful* thing—so far.

"I feel like I've been breathing in dirt instead of air," Jesse complained as he rooted through the box in front of him. "You think there's a soda machine around here?"

"If Erika *did* have a child, the child would be seventeen now, according to Mercer's theory," Aiden said, ignoring Jesse.

"Plenty old enough to go after Rae," Anthony said. They were on the right track. He could feel it.

Rae, Erika, Rae, Erika, Rae, Erika, he chanted to himself as he checked out the box he'd opened. That's all he was hoping to see. Something about Rae or Erika. But he got nothing. Aiden and Jesse must be having the same kind of crappy luck he was since neither of them was saying anything. Anthony shoved the box away. Opened another one. *Rae, Erika, Rae, Erika, Rae, Erika.* Nothing. He tore open another box. *Rae, Erika, Rae, Erika, Rae—*

"Yes," he muttered as he caught sight of Erika's name. "What do we got?" Medical charts. Useless. Copy of her birth certificate and driver's license. Useless. Copy of some work evaluation. Useless. *Man, did Mercer keep records of how many times she hit the head a day, too?* Anthony wondered. Copy of her income tax records. Useless. A picture of Yana's dad.

Wait. A picture of Yana's dad? What was a picture of Yana's dad doing in the box? He'd seen some pictures of Yana in the surveillance photos of Rae he'd found, which made sense because Rae and Yana used to hang together a lot. But Anthony was pretty sure Rae'd never met Yana's dad. The guy definitely wasn't the type to take his daughter's friends out for ice cream or anything like that. Anthony held the picture up to Aiden. "Any idea why—"

"You are not going to freakin' believe this," Jesse interrupted. His voice got higher with every word. He cleared his throat and rushed on. "This is from some notes Mercer wrote last week, the day before he died, I think. Anyway, it says he figured out who Erika's child was—Yana Savari."

"Yana?" Anthony repeated. *"Yana?"* Hot bile splashed up into the back of his throat. He'd kissed

Yana. Her hands had been all over him. He swallowed hard, but acid bile came right back up. Any second he could start to puke.

"Yeah, it says that Mercer thinks Erika never told Yana's dad about her being born," Jesse answered. "She left Yana with a friend in Oregon and came back here. But then after Erika died, when Yana was still really little, the friend got sick. She knew who Yana's dad was, and she took Yana to him."

"So we're saying Yana's the one after Rae?" Anthony said. He slapped the top of his head. Like that would get his brain functioning better or something. It was just so freaking unbelievable. How long had Yana been coming after Rae? When did she decide to get close to Rae by becoming her friend? He swallowed again, trying to keep from spewing.

"Yes," Aiden answered. He tightened the rubber band on his ponytail.

Anthony lurched to his feet. "I've gotta get to Rae. Right now."

Rae heard Yana's bedroom door swing open. "How did it . . ." Her words trailed off when she saw the expression on Yana's face. Make that the lack of expression. It was like Yana was wearing a mask.

"I have to get out of here. Right now." Yana

strode to her closet and pulled out a purple-and-yellow gym bag. "If I don't, I'm going to be locked away from now until God knows how long." She jerked open the top drawer of her dresser and shoved in some bras, panties, and socks.

"What? Where?" Rae couldn't even form a complete sentence.

"I know a place," Yana said. She pulled open the next drawer down and threw a couple of pairs of jeans, some T-shirts, and a sweatshirt into the bag. Then she turned to face Rae.

I was wrong, Rae thought. *Her face isn't like a mask. Well, it is, except for the eyes.* Yana's eyes were like blue fire, so intense that Rae expected anything Yana looked at to burst into flame. Including Rae herself.

"I need you to come with me," Yana said. "Please," she added before Rae could even form a thought. "Just for a few days, until I get myself settled."

"Of course. Yeah," Rae answered. What else could she say? *No, Yana. I've got a quiz in English, so I can't really help keep you out of the insane asylum right now.* And besides, it's not like she had a boyfriend who'd miss her or anything. "I just need to get some of my stuff and give my dad some kind of excuse so he won't flip out, then we're outta here to . . . wherever."

Yana dropped her gym bag and rushed over to Rae. She hugged Rae so tightly it hurt, and Rae could feel Yana trembling. "Thanks. Thanks, Rae," she said.

* * *

I can't stop trembling. I'm way too excited. It's finally going to happen. I'm finally going to kill Rae Voight. It is going to be like eating a whole box of Godiva chocolates at once, but slowly, one delicious piece at a time.

I've made Rae suffer a little—putting the "blood" on her clothes, spreading those flyers all over her school. But that's nothing compared to what I'm going to do to her when I get her away from here, away from Anthony, away from her daddy, away from anybody who can help her.

I can't wait until she realizes the truth. I can't wait until she knows that the only reason I ever pretended to be her friend was so that I could get close enough to hurt her the way I've been hurt. Finally I'm going to be able to make her pay for everything.

Chapter 9

Anthony forced himself to slow down as he turned onto Rae's street. He didn't want Rae's dad to see him driving thirty miles over the speed limit. Which he hardly ever did. But today he hadn't been able to stop himself.

"What are you going to say to him?" Jesse asked as Anthony pulled into Rae's driveway and parked.

"Come on," Anthony said, ignoring Jesse's question. He didn't have time to answer it. He might not have a second to spare. He strode up to the front door, rang the bell, then rang it again before he could stop himself. *Chill, all right?* he told himself. *You don't want to freak the guy out.* He jammed his hands in his pockets to keep from ringing the bell a third time—or ripping the door off its hinges with his bare hands.

"What are you going to—" Jesse began again. He was interrupted by Rae's dad opening the front door.

"Hello, Anthony," Mr. Voight said, smiling like he was actually glad to see Anthony. The guy was a college professor, but he always treated Anthony, well, basically like Anthony wasn't a moron. Like he was—like he was Marcus Salkow or something.

"Hey," Anthony answered, making sure to meet Mr. Voight's eye. He saw Mr. Voight glance at Jesse, and Anthony realized Rae's father was waiting for an introduction. *I would have already done that if I hadn't been raised by wolves,* Anthony thought. "Uh, this is Jesse Beven. He's a friend of Rae's, too. We were wondering if Rae was up for a movie."

"Rae had to go out of town for a few days," Mr. Voight answered. "Your friend, Yana? Her aunt died."

Anthony's intestines squirmed around like snakes. Yana. God, no. Was Rae with Yana?

"Rae wanted to go to the funeral with Yana since Yana's dad couldn't get off work," Mr. Voight continued. He ran his fingers over his bald spot, then seemed to realize what he was doing and put his hand in the pocket of his sweater.

"Where does Yana's aunt live? Do you have an address?" Anthony burst out. Mr. Voight raised an eyebrow.

"We might want to send a card. My mom, she says

everyone likes to know you're thinking about them when, you know, someone dies," Jesse jumped in.

Anthony's intestine snakes started biting each other at the word *dies*. *Rae's not going to die,* Anthony told himself. *You're not going to let that happen, even if that's what Yana has planned. Which maybe it isn't.*

"One second and I'll write it down for you," Mr. Voight said. "Do you two want to come in, have something to drink?"

"No, thanks," Anthony answered. "We should get going."

"Okay, be right back." Mr. Voight disappeared, leaving the door halfway open.

"What do you think Yana's going to do?" Jesse whispered. "I mean, what's she been waiting for all this time if she knew who Rae was?"

Good question, Anthony thought. "I think she might be kind of twisted," he answered. "Maybe she got off on being around Rae without Rae knowing who she was. Like I told you, she hooked up with me for a while just to stick it to Rae."

And now what? Now what's Yana's sick plan?

"Do you think—" Jesse said.

"Wait. He's coming back," Anthony cut him off, hearing Mr. Voight's footsteps heading in their direction.

"Here you go," Mr. Voight said as he stepped

back into the doorway. He handed Anthony a slip of paper. "I put the phone number on there, too."

"Great. Thanks a lot," Anthony said. He backed away from the door. "We've got to go or, uh, we'll miss the beginning of the movie."

"I hope it's a good one." Mr. Voight gave Anthony and Jesse a wave and shut the door.

Anthony bolted for the car. He pulled a map out of the glove compartment as Jesse got in the passenger seat. "You're not going to call first?" Jesse asked. "The aunt's house is supposedly in Louisiana. It'll take at least six hours to get there. And you don't know if that's where they're really headed."

"Yeah," Anthony answered, tracing a route with his finger. "But if I call and talk to the aunt—if there is an aunt. Yana might take off again as soon as she gets there. Anyway, it's better than sitting on my butt, wondering what's going on. It's a shot at least." Anthony tossed the map on the dashboard, then pulled out of the driveway.

"Shouldn't you be going left to get to the freeway?" Jesse asked.

"I'm dropping you at home first," Anthony said.

"No way. I'm going," Jesse protested, sounding more like Anthony's littlest brother than a fourteen-year-old.

"I need you here," Anthony answered. "I don't

know what I'm going to find in Louisiana. I need you and Aiden to keep digging around. Maybe Mercer knew something else about Yana, even what she had planned."

"Fine," Jesse muttered. He didn't say another word until Anthony came to a stop in front of his house. "Be careful, okay?" Jesse said. He didn't wait for an answer. Just climbed out of the car and slammed the door.

The car felt very empty without Jesse in it. Anthony cranked the music as he headed out. It didn't help much. His thoughts were too distracting. There was no way Yana would give Rae's dad a real address. Was there?

With Yana, who knew? Her aunt really could have died. And she could have brought Rae to . . . That's where Anthony got stuck. To what? To find some new way to torture her by pretending to be her best friend? That's what she'd been doing so far.

I'm probably going nuts over nothing. Yeah, Yana might make the next couple of days miserable for Rae, but that's it. And as soon as I find Rae and tell her the truth about Yana, it'll be over. Rae's tough. When she knows what the real deal is, she'll handle it. There's probably no reason for me to even be trying to track them down.

Anthony pressed his foot down on the accelerator.

His brain was telling him there was no real danger. But the gut snakes were telling him another story. He sped up a little more.

Steve Mercer was behind all the really bad stuff, he reminded himself, trying to keep calm. *He's the one who arranged for the pipe bomb that was supposed to blow Rae to bits. He's the one who kidnapped Jesse. He's the one who held Rae and Yana hostage. And he's dead. Yana's just doing kiddie stuff. Painting Rae's locker and putting those flyers all over school. Sick, yeah. But not lethal.*

You forgot the one where Yana started going out with you behind Rae's back, he thought. *And I actually helped her with that one. I'm such a moron.* Anthony pushed the accelerator down a little farther. *She's okay,* he thought. *She's okay. Yana's not going to do any damage.*

He told himself that over and over. Five hours and thirty-two minutes later he finally pulled onto the street that could or could not be where Yana's aunt lived. He parked a few houses down from what was supposed to be Yana's aunt's house. He didn't see Yana's yellow Bug anywhere. But maybe it was in the garage. Or maybe she wasn't even in this state.

Anthony checked his watch. It was almost two-fifteen. He wanted to go straight to the house, pound the hell out of the door, wake everybody up, then grab Rae and get her out of there. If she was in there, he couldn't help adding.

But that was a dumb plan. Yana was clearly wacked. And people who were wacked were unpredictable. It'd be better to wait until morning, then go up to the house and say he'd heard about Yana's aunt and decided to show up for the funeral. Then somehow he'd make sure Rae rode back to Atlanta with him. Yeah, that was what he should do and what he would do.

Anthony knew he could stretch out in the backseat for a while, nap. No one would be up and around for hours. But he also knew there was no way he was going to be able to force himself to take his eyes off the house. It was pointless to even try.

His eyes began to itch after about half an hour. A couple of hours later they began to burn. But he kept staring at the house, only blinking when he absolutely had to. Around five a girl on a bike threw a paper onto the porch. And a moment after that, the front door swung open. A woman in a robe stepped onto the porch.

Anthony launched himself out of the car. His feet had fallen asleep, and as he ran toward the house, he got the pins-and-needles sensation from his toes to his heels. He didn't care. "Hey," he called softly, not wanting to scare the woman. "Hi," he said as she turned toward him. "I'm a friend of Yana's. Are you one of her relatives?"

"I don't know who you're talking about," the woman answered, sounding sleepy and annoyed.

"Yana Savari," Anthony rushed on, even though he already knew the trip had been wasted. "Dyed blond hair. Blue eyes. About seventeen. Here for her aunt's funeral."

The woman shook her head as she headed back toward her door.

"Have you seen someone who looks like that around? Maybe I have the address a little wrong," Anthony called out.

"Haven't seen anyone like that," the woman answered. She ducked back into the house before Anthony could ask another question.

He stared at the closed door. There was no point in staying, but he couldn't get himself to leave right away. This had been his only hope of finding Rae. She and Yana could be anywhere. And he had no idea what that psycho Yana had planned.

"How long are you planning on staying here?" Rae asked Yana. She couldn't imagine surviving here even one more night. The hunting cabin was falling apart. She'd hardly slept at all the night before because she'd been afraid that part of the roof was going to come crashing down on her. And she'd found a mushroom growing on her faintly damp sleeping bag. It was a tiny, cute little mushroom, yeah. But it was still a mushroom.

"I don't know," Yana admitted. "But it's got everything I need." She wandered over to the steel sink in the kitchen part of the room—the cabin was all one big room, except for the bathroom, which in Rae's opinion shouldn't be called an actual room. It should be called gross-out central.

Yana turned the knob closest to her, and rusty brown water began to pour into the sink. "See? Running water. And an amazing knife—just like the ones from the commercials that come on at three in the morning." Yana picked up the blade and turned it back and forth, admiring it. "This baby can cut through a tin can."

"I don't know why you insisted on buying that thing. We didn't get anything at the store that needs cutting. We got peanut butter, bananas, bread—already sliced, thank you very much—American cheese—also already sliced, and each slice in its own little wrapper. We got—"

"I like my marshmallows thinly sliced," Yana interrupted. She gave a sheepish smile as she set the knife back down. "Besides, I don't know, it just makes me feel good to have it around."

"Safe, huh?" Rae said. Safety had to be at the top of Yana's list right now.

NO, I'M GOING TO USE IT TO SLICE OFF YOUR HEAD, RAE. YOUR NECK WILL BE MUCH EASIER TO CUT THROUGH THAN AN ALUMINUM CAN.

"Uh-huh. Safe," Yana answered. "Hey, you feeling all right?"

Yana's words sounded like they were coming from a million miles away. Rae could hardly hear them over the shrieks of her own thoughts. She hadn't been touching anything when she got that not-her thought. Nothing. But the thought had been so powerful, so *evil,* that it had almost knocked her off her feet.

"You feeling all right, Rae?" Yana repeated.

"Yeah," Rae managed to get out through a throat that felt like it was filled with itchy grains of dry sand. "Yeah."

YOU DON'T LOOK ALL RIGHT. YOU LOOK LIKE CRAP. BUT IT DOESN'T MATTER. THEY'LL PRETTY YOU UP AT THE MORTUARY. YOU'LL LOOK BEAUTIFUL, RAE. LIKE THE LITTLE PRINCESS YOU ARE.

I'm only losing my mind, she added silently. *'Cause what else could be happening?* Her psi ability was very specific. Touch fingerprint, get thought. So that horrible thought that had . . . had just raped her brain, it had to have come from something else. All Rae could think of was that it had come from herself, that she was schizophrenic or at least something like that.

PEOPLE WILL LIKE YOU A LOT MORE WHEN YOU'RE DEAD, RAE. MARCUS WILL PROBABLY EVEN CRY. THERE WILL BE ONE OF THOSE MEMORIALS AT YOUR LOCKER, WITH FLOWERS AND STUFFED ANIMALS AND EVERYTHING. YOU'RE GOING TO LOVE IT.

"So you have no idea where she is," Anthony pressed.

"Look, she goes off sometimes. I don't know where," Mr. Savari told him, his beefy body almost filling the doorway of the house. "Yana and I, we don't get in each other's business. She's seventeen. It's not like I need to be helping her cross the street."

Anthony glanced at Jesse. Jesse gave a little shrug. "When she shows up, will you just tell her I'm looking for her?" Anthony said.

"Sure," Mr. Savari answered. "I kind of thought she was with you, actually. She pretty much always is, right?"

"I guess." Anthony didn't see why he should tell Yana's dad that Yana'd used him like a Kleenex. "Later," he muttered. Then he turned and headed down the walkway to the sidewalk, Jesse right behind him.

"We have time to stop by her school before we're supposed to meet up with Aiden," Jesse said when they were back in the car. "Maybe one of her friends knows something."

Anthony glanced at his watch, then made a left when he got to the corner. "Might as well. There should still be some people hanging around. But I think Yana pretty much keeps to herself at school."

He cranked up the radio a little higher so he and Jesse wouldn't have to talk. Jesse always ended up asking some question like, "Do you think Rae's kind of like Yana's hostage?" Anthony hated it. It's not like he hadn't thought of whatever question Jesse spewed out. Almost every time, Jesse asked something that Anthony'd already been worrying about. But hearing the questions out loud made them feel twice as scary. Twice as *real*.

It only took about ten minutes to get to Yana's school. Anthony pulled into a parking spot and killed the engine. "Want to split up and meet back here in twenty?" he asked Jesse. "We can cover more people that way."

"I'll go right. You go left," Jesse answered.

Anthony climbed out of the car and headed left, which took him alongside the baseball diamond. He decided to try the weed-heads hanging out under the bleachers first. He always felt like he already knew guys like that even when he didn't. Probably because he'd spent the majority of his high school career as one of the guys like that.

"Hey," he said as he ducked under the bleachers, allowing himself a long suck of secondhand smoke. "I'm looking for Yana Savari." Every time he said her name, he got a dose of bile. The inside of his throat probably looked like raw hamburger. "Any of you know her?"

"That blond-headed chick who snarls if you try and talk to her?" a guy in a dorky monster-truck T-shirt asked as he tried to handle an almost nonexistent joint butt without a roach clip.

"Yeah. Sounds like her," Anthony answered.

One of the other guys carefully took the joint butt out of the monster-truck guy's hand and handed him a nice new fatty. "This is the last time I'm floating you," monster-truck guy's buddy warned. "You're always blowing all your cash and then looking all pathetic like it's my problem."

"Yana? Girl who snarls? Know where she is?" Anthony prompted. Monster-truck guy held the joint out to Anthony, but Anthony shook his head. Right now a few tokes would go down so good. But he'd be useless to Rae if he was stumbling around in a haze, obsessing about where he could find that chewy banana candy they used to have at the drugstore near his house. "Do. You. Know. Where. She. Is?" Anthony asked again, saying the words slowly and carefully.

"I hate that girl," monster-truck guy answered. Anthony looked at the other guys. There wasn't even a flicker of recognition in any of their bloodshot eyes.

"Guess I'll be moving on," Anthony said. He backed out of the bleachers and moved over to some marching band geeks taking a break. "Any of you know Yana Savari?"

"She's in my history class," a short girl holding a flute answered.

"You seen her around today?" *Say yes,* Anthony willed. *Say she's in the gym or in detention. Give me something here.*

"She skipped class. Again," the flute girl answered. "Big surprise."

"Any of the rest of you know where she might be?" Anthony pressed, even though he knew what the answer would be. He got the bunch of "nos" he was expecting—from the band geeks and everyone else he asked.

It was a thousand-to-one shot, anyway, he told himself as he headed back to the car. *Make that a million to one. Why did we even bother looking for Yana here? She and Rae are off . . . somewhere. You know that.*

He did know that. And the knowledge had turned his bones to cement, so heavy, every movement felt exhausting. But he had to keep looking, even in places where he was sure there'd be no chance he'd find Rae. If he didn't keep trying, he'd go nuts.

"Anything?" he asked as he got in the car. Jesse was already in the passenger seat.

"No," Jesse answered. "You?"

"No," Anthony said. He cranked the radio again and drove to the burger place where Aiden should be waiting for them. He spotted Aiden right away, sitting on one of the outside tables even though it was sort of too cold for it. "We came up with zip," he announced as he and Jesse joined Aiden at the table. "I think now we go to the cops."

Aiden picked at the table's peeling yellow paint. "Usually I'd say you were right. I'd say we come up with a convincing story and go to them right now."

"But?" Jesse asked, reaching for one of Aiden's fries.

"But it's almost a certainty that Yana has some kind of psychic power. I don't know what kind, but as the G-2s—the children born of the women who participated in the original group—reach adolescence, they have all begun showing abilities of some kind. Some stronger than others."

Knowing Yana, she's probably a freakin' power

genius, Anthony thought. *And it's not like Rae's power is going to give her a lot of help. It's not like she can make fire come out of her eyes or puke acid.*

"If the cops go in using conventional methods, they could get hurt, even killed," Aiden continued. "And we couldn't warn them. They wouldn't believe us."

"How dangerous can the powers be?" Jesse asked, stuffing a handful of fries into his mouth. As usual, he'd asked out loud the question Anthony really didn't want to hear.

"One of the G-2s is telekinetic. He can turn pretty much anything into a deadly weapon because he is able to hurl most objects, light or heavy, with phenomenal speed and accuracy," Aiden answered. "I'd say his powers are the most dangerous of those we know about. We, the agency, didn't even know Yana existed, so I don't have any data on her."

"And Rae?" Anthony couldn't help asking. "What kind of data do you have on her?" He was aware that now wasn't the time to speak in a voice laced with steel to the one person who could help him, but he couldn't help getting pissed off at the idea of this agency *tracking* Rae.

Aiden's eyebrows raised. "We were aware that she had, well, come into her abilities. The incident in her school last year and her subsequent stay in the hospital . . . She obviously has some power related to hearing others' thoughts. We hadn't narrowed it down to anything specific, however."

Anthony met Aiden's gaze directly, trying to read if Aiden was giving him the whole truth. Aiden stared back, challenging Anthony to push it further. Maybe even to tell Aiden what *he* knew.

"So what are we supposed to do now?" Jesse asked, returning Anthony's focus to the present.

"Yeah, it seems like we're up against a bunch of dead ends," Anthony said.

"I wish I could tell you you're wrong." Aiden carefully began placing his food wrappers into the empty takeout bag. "There's something else you should know."

Anthony knew it wasn't going to be good. He could hear it in Aiden's voice. "What? Just say it."

Aiden paused. "I unearthed another of Mercer's log books," he said. "It gave almost a moment-by-moment account of his days. As we thought, he hired someone to plant the pipe bomb that almost killed Rae. He had her under surveillance almost constantly after that. And he did hold her and Yana hostage in the Motel 6."

"But?" Anthony asked, twisting his hands together to keep himself under control.

"But Mercer wasn't the one who kidnapped Jesse," Aiden said, his gaze flicking over to Jesse.

"Going on the information we have, I'd say that the kidnapper was Yana."

"She could have killed him, keeping him in that warehouse," Anthony burst out. *Yeah, she could have,* he thought. *And it didn't matter to her at all.* Which meant Yana was capable of a lot more than stupid high school stuff. What was she doing to Rae right now? Was Rae even still alive?

She's alive, he told himself. *I'd know if she wasn't. I'd* know.

"We've got to find them. Right now. Today," Anthony said. He glared at Aiden. "You have to figure out how."

"I'll try. But I'll need to do more research," Aiden said.

Anthony pictured the boxes and boxes stuffed with paper. "We don't have time for that."

"I have an idea," Jesse blurted, his blue eyes glittering with excitement. "It might not work. But it might. It actually might."

Yana flipped a card, aiming for the pot she'd positioned in the middle of the floor. She missed. Again. The floor was covered with half the deck. The kings and queens and jacks all seemed to be staring at Rae, mocking her.

RAE IS CRA-ZY, RAE IS CRA-ZY, RAE IS CRA-ZY.

The thought singsonged through her head over and over. It wasn't hers. At least it didn't feel like hers, which didn't mean it wasn't some other personality or the kind of voice a psycho hears. Or maybe it was the playing cards. Maybe she was hearing their voices. Yeah. That made much more sense.

"Do we have any aspirin?" Rae asked. Yana didn't answer. *Did I say it out loud?* Rae wondered. *Or do I just think I said it out loud? God, I don't even know for sure.*

RAE IS CRA-ZY, RAE IS CRA-ZY, RAE IS CRA-ZY.

"You want to play cards?" Rae burst out, needing to talk to drown out the cruel voice inside her head and unwilling to ask the aspirin question again in case she already had.

"I am playing cards," Yana said. She flipped another card, zinging it so hard, it hit the opposite wall.

"I can see that," Rae answered through gritted teeth. "I mean do you want to play cards *with me*. Like hearts. Or crazy eights. Or go fish. Whatever, anything."

RAE IS CRA-ZY. RAE IS CRA-ZY. RAE IS CRAAAAA-ZZZZZZZY.

"It would be like we were in that book," Rae rushed on. "What was it called? *The Outsiders*. Ponyboy and this other guy were hiding out because one of them killed someone. And they spent their time playing cards and reading *Gone with the Wind* to each other. I loved that book."

"Sounds stupid. Two guys reading *Gone with the Wind*. That would never happen."

Flip, flip, flip went Yana's cards. *Crazy, crazy, crazy* went the not-her thoughts in Rae's head.

"Why are you being such a bitch?" Rae exclaimed. "I'm here because I'm trying to do you a favor. Do you even remember that?"

Zzzzy. Zzzzy. Zzzzy. Zzzzy.

The taunting thought had been shortened to a buzz, a buzz that competed with the pounding of Rae's headache. Yana flipped her last card, then she started crawling around the floor, gathering up the deck again.

"Did you hear me, Yana?" Rae demanded. She might be crazy. But not so crazy that she couldn't realize Yana was treating her like crap. For absolutely no reason.

Yana stopped crawling and sat down cross-legged across from Rae. "Okay, let's talk," she said. "What do you want to talk about?"

Rae shrugged. Something in Yana's tone made it seem like no answer Rae gave would quite work.

"I have an idea," Yana said. "Do you still want to know about my mother?"

"Yeah, sure, of course," Rae answered, trying to ignore the buzzing in her brain.

"Okay, well, you probably figured my mom ditched me and my dad, right?" Yana inched a little closer to Rae.

"Yeah. I didn't know for sure. But yeah, it seemed like what could have happened," Rae answered.

"Nope," Yana said. "My mother was murdered."

"Oh my God," Rae said, her eyes widening.

"Oh my God," Yana repeated, imitating her. She started cracking her knuckles. When she was done, she began working on her toes.

What was with Yana? It was like she couldn't sit still. And Rae couldn't decide if Yana wanted to keep talking to her or if she wished Rae hadn't come with her at all. Casually she brushed her fingertips over one of the cards Yana'd been flipping. The buzz in her head got louder. No thought wriggled its way through. *Another person's thoughts in my head is the last thing I need,* Rae told herself. *I just need to hang on, keep a grip on myself. I'll be okay. I've been okay all along. I never really needed to be in the hospital, and I don't now.*

"So aren't you going to ask me how it happened?" Yana asked, tilting her head from side to side to crack her neck.

"How did it happen?" Rae asked obediently.

"Her best friend did it," Yana said. "Can you believe it? That would be like you killing me. Or me killing you."

"That's . . . God, that's horrible," Rae replied. There was something about what Yana was saying—something familiar, like an echo in her brain. But it was hard to focus through the pounding and buzzing that filled her head.

"You're right!" Yana exclaimed. "It's completely freakin' horrible." She tried to crack her fingers again but couldn't do it. "And the only thing that would make it even a little better is if I could get revenge. But the woman who murdered my mom—the best friend—is dead."

Rae could feel her heartbeat in the veins of her forehead. Each beat brought a stab of pain. *Focus. Stay focused for Yana,* she told herself. *This is important.* "I guess death is a kind of revenge," she offered.

Yana gave a snort. She pushed the fingers of her right hand back. So far back.

"Yana, come on, stop. You're hurting yourself." Rae reached out and wrapped Yana's left hand in hers. Yana ripped it away.

"You don't understand at all," Yana shot back. Rae felt a light spray of spittle from Yana's mouth hit her on the cheek. "Someone dying isn't enough for revenge," Yana continued. "They have to suffer. Don't you get it? And you can't suffer when you're dead. But I found someone who could suffer." Yana slid even closer until her face was only inches away from Rae's. "Do you want to know who?"

Rae slid back a few inches, the rough wood floor snagging her pants. Yana was really starting to scare her. What if Dr. Hachin had been *right*? What if Yana really did need—

Yana leaned forward, and Rae's breath caught as she took in the expression on her face. "The murderer's daughter, that's who," Yana said. "You should see this girl, Rae. She has the perfect life. Perfect father. Perfect house. Even a housekeeper, if you can believe that. Plenty of money. You know the kind of girl I'm talking about."

She's talking about me, Rae realized, the pieces finally all fitting together in her head, even through the rest of the noise and pain. Yana was—Yana was Erika Keaton's daughter? It was too much, too much to understand. But Rae could see the hatred in Yana's eyes, and it all just made too much sense.

Now that I get it, what do I do? Rae thought, struggling to concentrate. *She brought me out here to—she must have brought me out here to kill me.*

"That really sucks," Rae said, trying to play dumb. "It must destroy you knowing that girl has it so good."

Her voice was shaking. She had to get it under control. Had to think of a plan. A way out of here.

"Yes!" Yana beamed at her. "Especially because my life is the absolute opposite. It's not fair. She's the daughter of the murderer. I'm the daughter of the victim. *I* deserve the perfect life."

"You do. You so do." Rae thought about suggesting that maybe Yana didn't know the whole truth about her mother's death. But that might infuriate Yana, and Rae really, really did not want to see Yana angrier than she was right this moment.

"I do," Yana repeated. She shoved herself to her feet. "I'll be right back. I've got to pee."

Thank God, Rae thought. *Thank you for giving me a chance.* As soon as the bathroom door shut behind Yana, Rae scrambled up. Keys. Where were the keys? Her headache was so bad, it was hard to keep her eyes open, but she scanned the room and spotted the keys on the counter by the sink.

Quickly, silently, Rae darted over to the counter and snatched up the keys. *Get out, get out now!* she ordered herself. With three long strides she was out the door of the cabin. She raced to the car, clambered inside, and jammed the key in the ignition. She didn't shut the car door. The first sound she wanted Yana to hear was Rae peeling out.

"Rae!"

Rae jerked her head toward the scream and saw Yana rushing toward her. She slammed the door and fired the engine.

DRIVE INTO THAT TREE!

That's not my thought, Rae told herself. She tried to slam the car in gear. Got it wrong. Tried again. Got it. Then she shoved her foot down on the gas. *I'm not even getting close to that tree. It's way out of the way.*

DRIVE INTO THAT TREE!

The thought hit her brain like a bullet. Rae's hands jerked the wheel to the left. Toward the tree. Her foot kept the gas pedal on the floor.

"No!" Rae cried. She tried to wrench the wheel to the right, but her hands wouldn't obey her.

DRIVE INTO THAT TREE!

Rae drove into the tree at full speed. And darkness surrounded her, pulling her into its depths.

Chapter 10

"So this scientist killed my mom?" Mandy Reese started making a tiny braid in one section of her long, light brown hair, concentrating on it like it was the most important thing in the world.

"Yes," Aiden told her. "I know how shocking this must be for you. I'm sorry to dump it all on you at once."

"Mandy can handle it," Jesse said. He slid his chair around Mandy's kitchen table to get a little closer to her. *He likes this girl,* Anthony realized. *I don't know if he knows it, but he definitely likes this girl.*

"Steve Mercer is dead now. I want you to remember that," Aiden said. "But when he was alive, it wasn't just the women in the group he was tracking." Aiden hesitated for a moment. Anthony could understand why. He wouldn't want to be the one who had to tell all of this to Mandy. "He was also tracking all the kids born to women in the group after they had received the treatment to boost their psychic abilities."

"Tracking," Mandy repeated. She began to twist the little braid she'd finished making around one finger. *That's gotta hurt,* Anthony thought. *She's doing it way too tight.* "So . . . watching me."

"Yes," Aiden said. "You, Rae, all the kids." This time Aiden didn't hesitate; his words came out in a rush. "It's because he believed that all of you would have powers, and he was right."

"But I don't have any powers. I don't," Mandy insisted. She tried to get her finger loose from her braid but only managed to get it more tangled. Jesse, blushing madly, reached over and gently slid the braid off her finger. "Thanks," Mandy said softly. "I'm always doing that. I don't know why I don't just stop." She turned her attention back to Aiden. "I really don't have any powers."

Aiden nodded. "Here's the thing. The powers don't express themselves until the height of puberty. We believe that a certain level of hormones in the bloodstream somehow activates the latent characteristic."

Come on, Aiden, speak English, Anthony thought. "Rae didn't get her power until last spring," he volunteered, shooting Aiden a quick glance. It was time to let Aiden in on everything. Maybe he already knew it, anyway. But Mandy had to know the whole deal, and that meant Aiden had to also.

"Rae? What? She didn't say anything," Mandy said.

"She doesn't tell most people because they freak," Anthony answered. Not exactly comforting for Mandy, he knew, but he kept going. "When she touches a fingerprint, she can—she can hear the thought the person who left it was having at that moment. Basically she can read fingerprints." Another look at Aiden revealed that the guy wasn't all that surprised. Or just had a lot of experience hiding the emotion. "It's kind of cool, actually," Anthony went on, wanting to try and hand Mandy something positive.

"So if I had something, would it be like that?" Mandy asked.

"There's no way of predicting what your talent will be," Aiden answered. "But it is almost certain that you will have one."

"And Aiden thinks he can bring it out earlier," Jesse jumped in. "He can inject you with something that will give you your power faster, and then you might be able to help us find Rae. I told them you'd be up for it."

"What?" Mandy cried. "Why would you tell them that? You don't even know me."

"We, you know, we talked on the phone a couple of times," Jesse muttered. "And I thought you liked Rae. This girl Yana could kill her, Mandy. Yana kidnapped me. That's how twisted she is. So, I'm serious, she really could kill Rae."

Anthony's eyeballs started to prickle. *You are not going to start bawling,* he told himself. *Not in front of everyone.* He gave a couple of hard blinks, then tried to concentrate all his attention on Mandy.

"What's in the injection?" she asked Aiden. Her face was pale, but her voice was steady. *She's handling all this a lot better than I would have at her age,* Anthony thought. *Or now.*

"It's an injection of the same kind of hormones your own body is already producing," Aiden answered. "The thing you have to know is that if you decide to take the injection, it will only be speeding up what will happen to you in time, anyway. The injection won't give you a power. It'll only bring out the power that would emerge sooner or later."

"And you really think if I do this, I can help you find Rae?" Mandy asked Jesse. Jesse was clearly the one she trusted.

"We don't know," Jesse admitted. "'Cause we don't know if whatever it is you'll be able to do . . . after is the kind of thing we could use to track Rae down. But it's pretty much the only shot we've got. That's why I brought these guys to you."

Mandy looked at Jesse for a long moment, and it was like they were continuing the conversation silently. "I'll do it," she finally said.

Aiden reached into the leather bag at his feet and pulled out a small glass bottle with a rubber stopper, a syringe, and a length of rubber tubing. Anthony noticed Mandy's eyes widen slightly, but she didn't say anything. She just stretched her arm out toward Aiden.

"I just need a second," Aiden told her. He slid the tip of the needle through the bottle's rubber stopper, then pulled back the plunger of the syringe. A few inches of the liquid in the bottle were sucked up. Aiden pulled the needle free and studied it. He gave the side a couple of taps with his fingernail. To get any air bubbles out, Anthony figured. "Okay, Mandy, I need you to make a fist," Aiden said after he'd tightened the rubber tubing around her upper arm. He ran his finger lightly over the inside of her elbow, tracing a vein. "You can still change your mind."

Mandy shook her head. Anthony bet her jaw was locked too tight to get out a word. He could see how tight the muscles there were.

"All right. Here we go." Anthony heard Jesse suck in a breath. And Anthony had to look away as the needle began to enter Mandy's delicate skin.

Rae opened her eyes, the world a blur of color around her. Slowly the colors separated and resolved themselves into the blue of Yana's sweatshirt, the white-blond of her hair, the brighter blue of her eyes. "You're awake," Yana said.

"You mean I'm conscious again," Rae muttered, meeting Yana's gaze unblinkingly.

"And I'm glad you are," Yana answered. "I was getting lonely. I can't wait to for us to start on all the fun things I've got planned."

GET A KNIFE FROM THE KITCHEN!

Rae instantly stood up from the floor of the cabin. "No." The word came out as a whimper, and Rae was disgusted for letting Yana get a glimpse of the fear raging around inside her.

"No, what? I didn't say anything," Yana told her.

GET A KNIFE FROM THE KITCHEN!

Rae's feet began to walk toward the counter. She could see the knife there, its blade shining in a spot of sunshine. *Don't pick it up,* she told herself. *You're stronger than she is. You're in control of your own body.* But her hand reached out and gently picked up the knife. Its handle was cool against her fingers. She knew Yana had touched the knife, but she didn't get any thoughts from it. *She must be able to block me somehow,* Rae thought.

"While you were *napping,* I was trying to decide on the best way to kill you," Yana said conversationally, like she'd been trying to decide which movie she and Rae should rent later. "I wanted something slow, so I was thinking maybe just hundreds of little cuts."

CUT THE BACK OF YOUR HAND! NOT TOO DEEP.

Rae tried to let the muscles in her fingers go slack. If she could just drop the knife, then— But even as she was thinking that thought, she started making a cut across the back of her left hand. A thin line of blood followed the path of the knife.

"That's one," Yana said. She sounded so happy. *She's doing this to me,* Rae thought. *It's impossible, but she's doing this to me.* "You look confused, Rae," Yana went on. "Did you think you were the only one who got a power from your mother? Mine is a pretty cool one, actually. I can put thoughts right into people's heads."

CUT THE BACK OF YOUR HAND AGAIN.

A moment later a second line of blood marred the back of Rae's hand. The tiny red droplets glistened all in a row, not big enough to roll down her hand. "Like I said, cool." Yana smiled. "I've been wanting to do this for so long."

"Since that day we met in the hospital?" Rae asked, her mind reeling. This was all too much to take in.

"That's right," Yana answered. "There was no community service assignment. I thought-implanted one of the administrators to get myself that job on the psycho ward. I wanted a chance to know the daughter of my mother's killer."

"You don't even know the truth about my mother," Rae said.

CUT YOUR HAND AGAIN!

Slice. Pain. More red droplets. Just like that. Rae's body obeyed Yana's thought commands so easily.

"I couldn't believe it when I figured out your powers," Yana said. "Could they be any more pathetic, Rae? You've got nothing to use against me. And you didn't even figure out what was going on with the witnesses when I kidnapped Jesse."

Rae raised her eyes from the thin lines of blood on her hand. "You did your thought thing on the witnesses," she said, the realization taking the air out of her. "That's—that's why they all had different versions of what happened."

"Weeks and weeks later, she finally understands," Yana said. "I knew you could get thoughts off prints when you were able to track Jesse down after you touched his pocketknife."

Rae shook her head. Too much, too much.

"I don't—you're obsessed with revenge because you think you've been treated so unfairly," Rae began. "But you have no problem hurting someone completely innocent, like Jesse. How does that work?" Maybe there was a way to get Yana to think about what she was doing in a different way. Maybe Rae could get her to see—

"Oh, come on. I didn't hurt little Jesse," Yana said. "You're the only one I want to hurt. And only because your mother is dead. If she were still alive, I'd go after her. You have to remember that everything I've done to you is your mother's fault. So don't blame me."

"There was never any chance that you were going to get institutionalized, was there?" Rae asked, the mind fog continuing to clear and revealing more and more frightening thoughts as it did. "That was a load of bull to get me out here with you."

"I thought-implanted my dad so you'd pick up the right info from his fingerprints," Yana explained cheerfully.

"And as a bonus, you decided to give me some of your implants to make me think I was losing it again," Rae said. "That was a good one. That really freaked me out."

"I know," Yana told her. "It was a great game. But the game is over."

MAKE A CUT ACROSS YOUR THROAT. NOT TOO DEEP.

Rae obeyed. "Yana, I never did anything to you. Can't you see that?" she cried.

MAKE ANOTHER CUT.

Rae didn't allow herself to make a sound as the knife bit into her flesh again. She wasn't going to give Yana the satisfaction.

"I wonder how many of these little cuts it will take to kill you," Yana said. "Thousands and thousands, I bet."

Mandy picked up the pencil off the kitchen table and flung it across the room. "That's the only way I'm going to make the thing move," she exploded. "I've concentrated until I feel like my head is going to crack open, and nothing!" Anthony noticed that her face was flushed and little drops of sweat had popped out all over her forehead. Was that from the hormone injection or just from how hard she'd been working? Aiden had been poking and prodding and testing the girl for hours. And Mandy had tried anything he asked without complaining. Until now.

"Can we stop?" she asked. "Whatever you did didn't work."

"You don't know that for sure," Jesse said.

"Yes, I do know," Mandy shot back. "It's my body, okay? In case you've all forgotten that." She tossed her long, light brown hair over her shoulders.

"Some of the emotion you're experiencing may be from the hormones," Aiden said gently. "Why don't we take a break, then try a few more things. I know we've done a lot of tests, but there are still psi abilities we haven't—"

"God, now I'm freezing," Mandy cut him off. "First I'm sweating like a pig, and now it's like I'm sitting on ice cubes or something."

"The physical effects will fade," Aiden promised her. Jesse grabbed a light blue sweater off the back of the chair next to him. He looked like he was thinking of wrapping it around Mandy's shoulders, but he just handed it to her instead.

"Thanks," Mandy said as she put it on. "I'm sorry, you guys. I—" She gasped, and her eyes opened so wide, Anthony could see the whites all the way around her irises.

"What's happening to her?" Jesse cried. Mandy's right hand was twitching, and Anthony could see the muscles in her throat moving up and down.

"I don't know," Aiden answered. He leaned close to Mandy. "Can you hear me? Mandy." He gave her shoulders a light shake, and Mandy shuddered, her eyelids fluttering.

"I saw my sister," she said, her voice trembling. "No, I *was* my sister. For a minute I was really her, Emma. I was sitting on Betsy Helf's bed—that's my sister's best friend—drinking a peach Snapple and trying to do a geometry problem."

Mandy jerked off the sweater. "This is hers, Emma's. Is that why it happened?"

"Very likely," Aiden answered. "I've seen a similar case."

"Case. Thanks," Mandy mumbled.

"I'm sorry. I didn't mean—" Aiden began.

"So you put on your sister's sweater and you *were* her. You saw where she was and what she was doing," Anthony interrupted Aiden, his eyes locked on Mandy. "If you could do that with something of Rae's, maybe we could track her down."

"Let's try it," Mandy said, still sounding a little dazed. "That was the point of this whole thing, right?"

"Are you okay to do it?" Jesse asked. "Do you need to rest?"

"No. We don't know what's happening to Rae. I can rest after," Mandy answered.

Tough little girl, Anthony thought. He liked her. Not as much as Jesse obviously did, but he liked her. "Come on. We'll take my car to Rae's, and I'll get something of hers." "I just need to write a note for my dad." Mandy grabbed a notepad off the counter by the phone, scribbled something, then stuck the note to the fridge with a magnet shaped like a doughnut. "Okay, ready."

Anthony led the way outside and over to his car. *We're going to find her,* he told himself as he started toward Rae's house. *She's going to be okay.* Jesse, Aiden, and Mandy talked a little on the ride, but Anthony didn't join in. All his thoughts were on Rae. It felt like it took forever, but about fifteen minutes later he pulled up in front of the Voights'. "Be right back," he said; then he jumped out of the car and ran up to the front door. He managed to ring the doorbell only once this time. Rae's dad seemed surprised to see him.

"Hi. I know Rae's still out of town, but I realized I left a book in Rae's room when she was helping me study," Anthony said, speaking so quickly, his words almost slammed into each other. "You mind if I go get it? Test tomorrow."

"You know the way," Mr. Voight said. He stepped back and let Anthony into the house.

"Thanks," Anthony said over his shoulder as he rushed down the hall. He burst into Rae's room and grabbed a sweater out of the hamper in her closet. He wasn't sure if Mandy needed something that had been worn recently, but he figured it couldn't hurt.

"Thanks again," Anthony called as he bolted out of the house with Rae's sweater stuffed under his shirt. He heard Mr. Voight call something in reply, but he was going too fast to register exactly what. Didn't matter. He had to get the sweater to Mandy so he could get to Rae.

"Here you go." Anthony climbed in the car, slid the sweater out from under his shirt, and passed it to Mandy. She cradled it to her chest. "Do you need to put it on?" he asked.

But Mandy was already gone, her eyes wide and staring. She brought her right hand up to her throat and made a slicing motion. And then she screamed, the sound bouncing off the walls of the car and jolting through Anthony's bones.

Jesse jerked the sweater away from Mandy. "Hey, Mandy, Mandy. You're okay. You're sitting in the car with me. With us," he corrected himself.

Mandy's eyelids did the fluttering thing, then Anthony could see her come back into her body. It sounded weird, but that was how it looked to him. "What?" he asked, struggling to keep the urgency out of his voice. "What'd you see? Did you see Rae?"

"I *was* her," Mandy answered. She rubbed her neck with both hands. "And you guys, Rae was trying to kill herself. We—she—had a knife in her hand, and she was cutting her throat."

"Rae wouldn't do that. No way," Anthony burst out.

"Did you see Yana?" Jesse asked.

"Yeah. She was there. Just watching Rae. She wasn't doing anything to stop her," Mandy answered. "But it wasn't Yana holding the knife. It was definitely Rae."

"Can you remember anything that would tell us where she was?" Aiden asked.

Mandy shook her head. "I saw a section of a beat-up place, a cabin, I think. But that's it." She picked up the sweater. "Let me try once more—"

And she was gone again. Anthony stared at her throat, praying he wouldn't see that slicing motion again. It took him a few seconds to realize that this time Mandy's feet were moving. Jerking back and forth. Then Mandy's breath started to come in harsh pants.

Aiden pulled the sweater out of her grasp. "I was running," Mandy said when she'd recovered. "I mean, Rae was running. Running down a rutted dirt path. She got away somehow."

"What did you see? Anything could be important. A kind of tree. A car. Anything," Aiden told her.

"I climbed over a fence. Then I fell. I was looking up at the fence. I mean *Rae* was looking up at the fence." She shook her head, obviously still overwhelmed by what was happening to her. "There was a sign on it," she went on. "It said 'private property.'"

"That's it?" Anthony burst out. He didn't mean to sound angry, but he did. Mandy didn't seem to notice. Or she didn't care.

"There was a name, too," she continued. "Morton. But that's it. That's all I saw."

Chapter 11

Rae found herself staring up at Yana for the second time. God, she hated that, seeing Yana smirking down at her. She wished she could claw the little smile right off Yana's face. Of course, she couldn't move. Not a muscle. One of Yana's thought implants had taken care of that.

"Very good escape attempt, Rae," Yana said. "I'm impressed. I didn't think you had the upper-body strength to make it over the fence. Guess you had a real adrenaline rush going, huh?"

Rae wouldn't have answered even if she had control of the muscles in her lips and tongue. What was the point?

"I think we'll stay out here for a little while so you can enjoy the beautiful day, your last day," Yana went on. "Nobody ever comes down that road, so we'll have the place to ourselves. Then when you get hungry, we'll go inside and I'll fix you lunch. I found a yummy box of rat poison under the sink."

Rae felt tears sting her eyes. She wanted to blink them away—she didn't want Yana to see—but she didn't even have the muscle control to do that. All she could do was lie at Yana's feet. Paralyzed. Helpless. As good as dead.

Anthony climbed the chain-link fence. Then he followed the bumpy dirt road, keeping under the cover of the trees alongside it. *She's going to be here,* he told himself. *Yana won't have moved her because there's no way Yana can know that we uncovered the location of her cousin's hunting cabin.* Once Mandy had gotten the name Morton, Aiden had used his "source," whoever that was, to do the rest.

"Score," he whispered when he rounded a bend in the road and saw Yana's VW Bug. It was parked in the shade across from a cabin that looked like it could be reduced to splinters if you breathed on it too hard. As he looked closer, he noticed a big dent in the front of the Bug. It looked like Yana had plowed the thing head-on into something very big, and very heavy. Was Rae in the car when that happened? Mandy hadn't said anything about a car or an accident. . . .

Focus, he commanded himself. He had to get to that cabin. Crouching as low as he could, Anthony crossed the clearing in front of the cabin and positioned himself under one of the windows. It was a pretty big one, which was kind of weird for such a crummy little place. But Anthony wasn't complaining. He wanted to see as much as he could. Maybe he'd even get an idea what Yana's power was. That would be *helpful.* He wasn't loving the idea of trying to get Rae out of there without knowing what Yana could do.

Anthony raised his head just enough to look into the window. The first thing his eyes found was Rae. He checked her neck. There were a bunch of scratches running across it. They could have been made with a knife, but only if it was used with almost no pressure.

He let out a breath he hadn't realized he'd been holding. Then his ribs collapsed against his heart. Rae had picked up a spoon and was digging it into a box of rat poison. She was going to eat it.

He didn't think. He didn't plan. He let his body do the thinking. Anthony charged to the door of the cabin and yanked on it. Locked. He wheeled around and moved into position a few feet from the big window. He could see Rae and Yana staring at him. He didn't care. He ripped off his shirt, wrapped it around his head, then blindly launched himself at the window. He landed hard on the cabin floor, glass raining down around him.

Before he could stand up, Rae was at his side. "Are you okay?" she cried, her voice trembling.

"I'm fine. And I'm getting you out of here." Anthony got to his feet without slicing his hands to pieces on the glass. He thought he had a few cuts here and there, but who cared? He'd found Rae. He reached out and took her by the hand. "You going to try and stop us?" he asked Yana.

"No," Yana answered. But she was smiling. What did she have planned? Didn't matter. Anthony took a step toward the door, pulling Rae with him.

STOP! BRING HER TO THE TABLE!

The thought was so forceful that Anthony's body jerked. "What?" Rae demanded. He didn't answer. He picked her up in his arms. Then he turned away from the cabin door and started walking toward Yana.

THAT'S RIGHT. BRING HER TO THE TABLE AND PUT HER BACK IN HER CHAIR.

"Anthony, no!" Rae shouted. "Yana's controlling you. Can't you feel it?"

God, Rae was right. Anthony hadn't even realized

the thought that had gotten his body moving wasn't his own. He tried to stop his legs from moving, but it was like the wires running between his brain and body had been cut. He had a new brain. Yana's brain.

Rae began to struggle, twisting in his arms. *Yeah, do it. Get away,* he thought, the sound of his own inner voice a whisper compared to the commands he'd gotten from Yana.

HOLD HER TIGHTER!

Anthony's arms immediately cinched closer around Rae. She bucked and squirmed and kicked. But she wasn't anywhere near as strong as he was. He kept walking until he reached the chair Rae'd been sitting in when he peeked through the window. He set her down and held her in place.

TIE HER UP! TIE HER TIGHT!

Anthony scanned the room for something to use as binds. "Looking for this?" Yana asked as she tossed him a length of rope.

"Don't, Anthony. Don't do it. You're stronger than she is," Rae told him.

But he wasn't. He was a puppet. And Yana had her hand inside him, controlling every move. Methodically he tied Rae's feet to the bottom of the chair, then he brought the rope up and laced her torso to the chair rungs. He heard her give a little gasp of pain as the rough rope bit into her. He jerked the rope tighter. He had to.

"Good boy, Anthony," Yana said. "Now it's time to feed Rae. Take that box of rat poison and make her eat a nice big spoonful!"

FEED HER THE POISON!

Anthony focused all his mental energy on keeping his hands at his sides. He could feel his muscles twitching with the effort of resisting. But still he grabbed the box and scooped out a heaping spoonful of the poison. Then he crouched down next to Rae and brought the spoon to her lips. She twisted her head away. He followed with the spoon.

FORCE HER MOUTH OPEN!

With his free hand Anthony grabbed Rae's jaw and pried open her mouth. His heart screamed as he brought the poison to her open mouth. *I'm going to kill her,* he thought. *I'm going to kill Rae.* He felt something hot and wet run down his face and realized he was crying.

Rae tried to lock her teeth, but Anthony's grip was too strong. She could smell the bitterness of the poison, almost taste it. *I'm going to die. Right now. I'm going to die.*

She locked eyes with Anthony. His face was what she wanted as her last memory. A salty ball formed in her throat as she realized there were tears streaking down his cheeks. *Look at me,* she willed him. *Look into my eyes. I understand. It's not your fault.*

I love you.

The thought exploded inside her with a rush of heat. She could practically feel her veins glowing gold. She loved him. Let him see it. Let him know.

Rae felt the cold metal of the spoon against her teeth. This was it. She closed her eyes, trying to hold on to the vision of Anthony's face, not tightened into a grimace, the way it had been as he strained to keep from hurting her, but smiling, his melted-Hershey eyes bright.

Something hit the floor with a thud. A moment later there was a clatter. Then Rae felt the rope wrapped around her body loosening. She snapped open her eyes and saw Aiden, Jesse, and Mandy come bursting through the door. Yana lay on the ground. And Anthony was ripping the rope off her.

"What happened?" she exclaimed.

"Aiden got Yana with a tranquilizer dart," Jesse exclaimed.

"Is she knocked out?" Anthony demanded.

"Yeah," Aiden answered.

"We have to keep her that way," Anthony said. "She can put thoughts in your head. Make you do whatever she wants."

"I'll take care of it," Aiden answered.

"How?" Anthony demanded. "How are you going to stop her from coming after Rae?"

"I'll take her to a safe place and keep her sedated until I find a way to block her power. There are various barrier substances that could work," Aiden answered. "When she's ready, I'll tell her that Rae's mother didn't kill her mother. Then there'll be no reason for her to ever go after Rae again."

"And you think she'll believe you?" Anthony asked. "You're going to tell her the lame junk you told me? That Rae's mom just didn't have the personality type to be a killer? 'Cause Yana's not ever going to buy that." Anthony strode up to Aiden. "I think there's a lot that you're not telling us. Yana's going to need to hear the whole story. And so do we—*now*."

Rae let out a slow breath, enjoying the feeling of having someone stand up for her. "Do you have some kind of proof?" she asked Aiden as she pushed herself to her feet. "I know my mom didn't kill Erika. But do you know what happened?"

"Tell her now," Anthony insisted. "Tell her whatever you're going to tell Yana that's going to convince her."

Aiden stared down at Yana's limp body for a long moment, then he raised his eyes to Rae. "I'll tell you the truth if you want me to. But it's dangerous for you to know. Any of you."

"Tell me," Rae answered. Aiden, Jesse, and Mandy all nodded. "Tell us," Rae added.

"I know for an absolute fact that your mother didn't kill Erika Keaton because Erika was killed by one of the government agents."

"Why?" Rae cried.

"She was horrified by what had been done to her and the women in the group—and what could happen to their children. She decided to go public. And she was stopped."

"Murdered," Anthony bit out. "Use the right word. She was murdered."

"Murdered," Aiden agreed.

"How did my mother even get connected to Erika's death, then?" Rae asked. "She was Erika's best friend."

Aiden's eyes skittered away from Rae's face. "She got connected because the agency wanted her to be connected."

"You bastards framed her," Anthony cried.

Rae reached out and used the kitchen table to steady herself. She knew her legs were too weak to hold her up. "Is that what happened?" she asked Aiden.

"Yes," he said, his voice coming out choked. "The agency planted evidence to implicate your mother. I didn't know about it at the time. I was very new, just out of college. But I got the details later. There were fears that Melissa might also try to go public. Framing her took away any credibility she might have. She did try to tell the truth—and that's why she was found unfit to stand trial."

"And that's why she was put in the mental hospital," Rae said. The floor felt like it was softening under her feet, softening and rolling. She'd trusted Aiden. When would she learn to stop trusting people? "I don't understand why Steve Mercer killed my mother, then," she said. "It made sense when he thought what he'd done to her had turned her into a murderer. He told me he killed her to stop her from killing anyone else. But he must have known the agency killed Erika and not my mother."

Aiden shook his head. "No, Rae. Steve Mercer was on the run from the agency himself at that point. He believed the evidence we—the group," he quickly corrected himself, "planted. He did kill your mother because he thought she'd become dangerous."

Aiden turned to Mandy. "He killed your mother for the same reason," he said. "Apparently, she had recently been involved in an altercation with a coworker who consequently became the victim of a tragic accident on the job. Steve must have suspected your mother was responsible, despite evidence to the contrary." He coughed. "Mercer really lost it," he said, almost to himself.

A long silence filled the room. There were so many questions fighting for attention inside Rae that she couldn't focus on one long enough to ask it.

"What was my mom's—what could she do?" Mandy finally blurted out. "I mean, why would Steve think she could have killed that person?"

Rae glanced at her, hearing the tremor in Mandy's voice. Poor Mandy had found out so much all at once—at least the truth had come more slowly to Rae. It had been beyond frustrating not to know everything, but still. It was a whole lot to know.

Aiden cleared his throat. "Amanda—your mother— could draw out people's deepest fears," he said. "Before her involvement in the group, she'd apparently been particularly intuitive in this area. After the, uh, the treatments—she was quite skilled at picking up on the slightest cues about what most terrified someone. Therefore, the unfortunate accident at their office must have been particularly suspicious to Mercer."

"People's fears," Mandy breathed, her eyes wide with shock. "She could see people's fears."

Rae tried to meet Mandy's gaze, pass on some kind of support, but Mandy looked away. It was like she was lost in some other place, trying to make this information fit into the memories she had of her mother. And Rae knew just how personal and private that connection could be.

"I guess I'll . . ." Aiden let his words trail off. He knelt down and lifted Yana into his arms, then headed out the door. Mandy started after him, signaling to Jesse to follow.

Then Rae was alone with Anthony. She took a wobbly step toward him. He rushed to meet her, grabbing her under both elbows. "Nasty bump you got there," he said.

"Yeah," Rae answered. "I guess I can tell my dad it was another volleyball injury. I can say one of the girls on the other team had a monster spike." She glanced down at her hands. "At least I can cover the cuts with makeup."

"Yeah. That should work," Anthony said.

Why are we having this stupid conversation? Rae wondered. All she wanted was to feel his arms around her. Didn't he know that?

A second after the thought went through her head, her wish was a reality. He felt warm against her—warm and safe.

"Don't let go, okay?" she murmured against his neck.

"I won't," he answered.

That was all she needed to hear.

* * *

Rae cracked open her fortune cookie. "Serenity is your special gift," she read aloud to Mandy. Mandy cracked up. It was good to hear her laugh. God, on the day that Rae got her powers, she was completely terrified. Although it wasn't like Mandy's introduction to the wonderful world of psi abilities had been a day at the beach.

"I told you thanks, right?" she asked.

"About a million times," Mandy answered.

"Well, let's make it a million and one," Rae said. "Thank you. Thank you so much."

"You're welcome," Mandy answered. "You don't have to stay and baby-sit me, you know. I'm really okay."

"I'm not baby-sitting you," Rae insisted. "I want to be here. That was really intense today. It's good to be with someone who was there."

"Wouldn't you rather be with Anthony?" Mandy asked. She split open a fortune cookie and folded up the fortune without reading it.

Yeah, I would rather be with Anthony, Rae thought. But she wasn't going to tell Mandy that. No matter what Mandy said, Mandy needed to be with someone who had a clue what she was going through. And that was Rae.

"I can see Anthony at school tomorrow," Rae said, attempting and, she thought, achieving a sincere tone.

Mandy flopped back on her bed, then sat up and pulled a pizza box out from under her shoulders. She tossed it on the floor, then stretched back out again. The girl was not a neat freak. That was for sure.

"How weird is it knowing so much about other people?" Mandy asked, staring up at the ceiling.

"Extremely weird," Rae answered. "It's enough just to deal with the stuff going on in your own life, you know?"

"Yeah," Mandy answered.

"I don't know if this would work for you 'cause I don't know if you're getting your info through your hands, but I keep a wax coating on my fingers pretty much all the time. That way I only get junk on other people when *I* decide I want to," Rae explained. "It helps to find a way to be in control like that. If you want, the two of us can work on figuring out a system for you."

"That would be great," Mandy answered. "But not tonight." She yawned. "I'm dead." She gave an embarrassed giggle. "Sorry."

"No worries," Rae said.

"I guess it's different for Yana." Mandy rolled onto her side and looked at Rae. "She always has control. Nothing's getting zapped into her head. She's the one that does the zapping."

"Yeah. God, I don't even know what to think

about Yana," Rae admitted. "She tried to kill me. But she's spent years believing my mom killed her mom. That's enough to warp anyone."

"My mom was murdered, too. So was yours," Mandy reminded her.

"Yeah, but I've only known that for a little while," Rae answered. "And you . . . Well, did you ever feel like you wanted to track down the carjacker—the supposed carjacker—who killed your mom?"

"It seemed pretty impossible," Mandy said. "But . . . yeah. I guess I wanted him to pay somehow. A couple of times the cops thought they'd found the guy, and—" Mandy stopped. She shook her head. "Now I know who killed her, and I also know he's dead. It's like too much information in one day."

"You gone all numb?" Rae asked.

"Yeah." Mandy started to nibble on one of her fortune cookie halves, getting crumbs all over the bed. "You think Aiden will be able to convince Yana that the government guys killed her mother and that your mom had nothing to do with it?"

Rae let out a long sigh that felt like it started all the way down in her stomach. "I hope so. But it's kind of hard to believe. The whole thing is hard to believe."

Mandy sighed, too, a deep sigh that sounded a lot

like Rae's. "I guess there's no point in telling my sister or my dad the truth about what happened to my mom."

"It's up to you," Rae answered. "I didn't tell my dad. I . . . it's a pretty hard thing for people to handle. And . . ." Rae hesitated, but she wanted to be honest with Mandy. "And I thought if I told him about my powers, he'd want to get me some kind of help. I was afraid I'd end up in the hospital again or some kind of research facility. That's not where I want to spend my life."

"Me either." Mandy tossed her partially eaten cookie in the trash. Or toward the trash. She missed, but she didn't seem to care. "It's like our whole lives got stolen. Yours, mine. Even Yana's."

Rae reached over and squeezed her shoulder. "Not our whole lives. And even though it's all kind of twisted, Mercer did give us something, too. Not that we should be grateful," she rushed to add. "But there are some things I've done with my fingerprint thing that I feel pretty good about. That's something, I guess."

"Yeah." Mandy yawned again.

"I should call my dad to come pick me up," Rae said. "You're falling asleep on me."

"No, I'm not," Mandy protested. Then she yawned so wide, her jaw cracked.

"Yes, you are. I'm going to go. But you're not going

to get rid of me for long," Rae promised. "It's like, I don't know, you're my honorary little sister now."

Mandy smiled back at her, and Rae felt some warm fuzzies inside her. And she didn't even feel the least bit dorky for it.

Anthony checked the clock in the Hyundai's dash. "Almost time for the first bell," he told Rae. He wished there were hours to go. Days. Sitting here in the private world of the car, breathing in the warm citrusy smell that was part perfume and part pure Rae, was all he needed to be happy. "You okay with going in there?"

"Because of the mom thing?" Rae asked. Anthony nodded. "After almost eating rat poison, facing down a little high school gossip is no biggie."

Anthony suddenly felt like *he'd* been eating rat poison, like it had eaten through his stomach—hot and acidic—and was starting to work on the rest of his body. "I should have been able to hold out against her," he muttered. "I should have—"

"Shut up," Rae said, her voice gentle. "Nobody could have held up against Yana. Even Aiden isn't going to let her regain consciousness until he figures out some kind of barrier that will keep her from inputting thoughts into his head."

"You think she's the strongest?" Anthony asked.

It was the question he'd spent most of the night asking himself.

"I don't know. I don't even know how many of us are out there," Rae answered, her eyes darkening. "But knowing there are more, that I'm not the only one . . . I wonder if I'll ever meet them. It's scary to think about. I can almost see why Steve Mercer went insane and did what he did. If you thought that something you created was so dangerous, it makes sense that—"

"What he did to your mom doesn't make sense, Rae," Anthony interrupted. "The guy was deranged. If he wanted to protect people, he should have swallowed a bullet before he started doing his experiments."

"Yeah. I'm never going to stop hating him for what he did to my mother," Rae acknowledged. "And to Mandy's mother, too. But I really can see how he got obsessed with eliminating everyone who might use their powers in ways that could hurt people. How can anyone be safe with us walking around alive? With these abilities that—"

"Not all of them—you—are going to be Yanas," Anthony reminded her, wanting to reach over and smooth away the crease that had appeared between Rae's eyebrows but wrapping his hands around the steering wheel instead. "Some will be Mandys. And Raes."

"But are the Raes and Mandys going to be enough to keep the Yanas from . . ." Rae let her words trail off.

"If they have the help of the Anthonys and the Jesses and even the Aidens, then yeah, definitely. We're the stronger team," Anthony said. The bell rang, and he reached for the door handle.

"Anthony," Rae said, her voice loud in the interior of the car.

"What?" he asked.

"Do you think . . . ?" Rae's eyes lowered, refusing to meet his.

"Do I think what?" Anthony pressed.

"Do you think you might ever want to kiss me or put your arms around me or anything when you haven't just saved my life three seconds before?" Rae blurted, finally looking right into his eyes.

Did she want him to . . . ? Wait. Was she asking? Anthony felt like, like . . . He couldn't even describe it. Like he'd swallowed a skyful of stars.

He reached out and took Rae's face in his hands. His fingers were trembling, and he hoped she didn't notice. "Yeah," he said, his voice coming out all husky. "I think I might want that." And he lowered his lips toward hers. It wasn't the first time they'd kissed, but it was the first time he'd actually had time to think about it. To realize exactly what he was doing. *I'm kissing Rae Voight,* he thought as his lips brushed against hers. And this time he allowed himself to feel the rush of emotion that came with that thought.

He raised his head. He needed a moment. He actually felt dizzy from that tiny bit of contact. He caught a flash of movement out of the corner of his eye, then realized Marcus Salkow—totally oblivious to him and Rae—was walking by the car.

That's the kind of guy Rae should—

No. Anthony stopped himself midthought. Salkow didn't deserve Rae. The weenie couldn't even stand by her when the truth came out about her mom.

"What?" Rae asked.

Anthony shook his head. "Nothing. I was just thinking how I really want to kiss you again."

Rae smiled. "So what's stopping you?"

"Absolutely nothing," Anthony answered.

turn the page
for a preview of
fingerprints #7:

Rae Voight had an impulse to stop dead in the middle of the hallway, fling her arms out wide, and cry, "Just look, okay? Just take a good long look and stop giving me all those sneaky out-of-the-corner-of-your-eye glances."

But she didn't. When everyone at school recently found out your mother was a murderer who died in a mental hospital and everyone already knew that you had spent your summer vacation in, yes, a mental hospital, it wasn't that smart to draw *more* attention to yourself.

Except . . . at this point, all of that barely seemed to matter. How bizarre was that? The possibility that even her best friend might find out the truth about Rae's mom used to be Rae's biggest fear. And now everybody knew. She was sure even the janitor had heard. She was sure the AV guys, who usually didn't talk about anything except how bad they wanted a plasma TV, were gossiping about her. And she cared . . . some. That's it. She wasn't even close to being destroyed the way she'd always thought she would be if anyone found out about her mom.

Maybe it was because she knew her mother hadn't killed anyone. She'd been convinced of that ever since she'd touched a letter with her mother's fingerprints on it and used her psychic ability to pick up the thoughts her mom had been having when she wrote the letter. But now she had proof—Aiden's confession. Aiden had finally admitted to Rae that her mom had been set up to take the blame for her best friend's death. Rae wasn't the daughter of a killer.

And she also wasn't being stalked by her *own* best friend anymore. Yana Savari had turned out to be the one after her all along, but now Aiden had Yana tucked away somewhere she couldn't hurt Rae.

So her mom was innocent, and Rae was safe. But even with all of that, the other major reason why Rae didn't really care what anyone here in school thought of her was that Anthony Fascinelli had kissed her— kissed her until her lips got all puffy and sore in a good way. Who could care about anything after that? The kiss hadn't even been after a crisis situation, either. He hadn't kissed her because she'd almost died.

Or because he almost had. So it totally counted. A little smile broke across Rae's face as she thought about the kiss and all the kisses that had come after that kiss in the past week. The smile earned her a few more what's-your-deal looks. Clearly people thought Rae should never smile again now that the so-called truth about her mom was out. But forget them. She had to smile. 'Cause school was over for the day, and as soon as she found Anthony, they'd be kissing again.

As if her thoughts had conjured him up, Rae felt Anthony's hands slide around her waist. She twisted around to face him, impatient to feel his mouth on hers, to become RaeAnthony instead of Rae and Anthony. They'd kissed hundreds of times in the week since *the* kiss, but Rae still felt starved for the taste of him. When his lips met hers, God, it was like everything she'd ever wanted in her whole life had been dumped in a pile at her feet with a big bow and whipped cream and a cherry on top.

"Car," Anthony said into her mouth, and he started backing her down the hall without breaking the kiss. Rae locked her arms around his shoulders and easily matched her steps to his. No, it wasn't even like she was trying to match him. When they were RaeAnthony, her body and his body moved together perfectly, like they were two halves that had been rejoined as soon as Rae and Anthony kissed.

They made it out of school and to Anthony's Hyundai without breaking contact. Anthony backed Rae up against the passenger side door, then slowly, reluctantly slid one of his hands off her body. Rae heard the jangle of keys, then she felt Anthony fumbling to unlock the door behind her. *Wonder how many times I can make him drop them today?* she thought. She eased away from him, just the tiniest bit, and traced the curve of his upper lip with her tongue.

And the keys hit the asphalt. Rae loved that she could do that to Anthony—make him tremble so bad, he couldn't keep his grip on a set of keys. Of course, he could do it right back to her, which she loved just about as much.

Anthony bent her back at the waist—like a tango dancer—as he leaned down to retrieve the keys. There wasn't a fraction of an inch of space between their bodies. Rae opened her eyes, needing to look at Anthony. His eyes, his melted-Hershey's-Kiss brown eyes, opened a second later. It was like that with them. They were so in sync. RaeAnthony. AnthonyRae.

"Got 'em," Anthony said, his lips sliding off hers and onto her cheek. He straightened up, pulling Rae with him.

"Anthony," she gasped.

He gave her a shy smile, about to lean in for another kiss.

"No, Anthony," Rae blurted as she tightened her hands on his shoulders. She could feel her nails starting to dig into his skin, but she couldn't loosen her grip. "There's someone in the backseat of the car," she said, a familiar waver entering her voice. One week. She'd gotten one week free of fear, and now it was all rushing back. "On the floor," she managed to get out.

Anthony jerked his head toward the back window, already pushing Rae behind him to make his body a kind of shield for her. Rae held her breath, and then Anthony looked back at her, reassurance in his eyes. "It's Aiden," he told her.

Rae let out a shaky sigh of relief. Aiden Matthews had saved her life more than once. If that didn't mean she could trust him, what did? Anthony unlocked Rae's door, and she climbed in. "Don't look at me," Aiden ordered. He repeated the instruction when Anthony got behind the wheel. "Just drive," he continued. "Not fast. It should look like the two of you are just off to the mall or wherever it is you go."

"What's wrong?" Anthony demanded as he pulled out of the parking space and headed out of the lot.

"Yana escaped," Aiden answered.

Rae felt like her blood had been replaced by novocaine. Her body went all thick and heavy . . . and dead. "Yana," she whispered, her tongue stumbling over the name.

Anthony reached over and grabbed her hand. She could barely feel the warmth and strength of his fingers. "Nothing's going to happen to you," he said fiercely.

Rae flashed on the cabin, the cabin where Yana— Yana who had been her very best friend less than a month ago—had taken Rae to kill her. Rae saw herself holding a knife, being forced by Yana's thought-implanting ability to run it across her throat, lightly, lightly. Yana had wanted Rae to die slowly. She'd wanted to watch Rae suffer. And now Yana was out there somewhere. And what else would she be doing but coming after Rae, wanting to make sure Rae ended up dead this time?

"Did you tell Yana the truth?" Anthony asked, glaring at the road in front of him. He jerked the car to a stop at a red light. "Did you tell her that Rae's mom didn't kill her mother? Did you tell her that it's your friggin' secret government agency she should be going after?"

"It was never *my* agency. And I'm not a part of it anymore," Aiden answered.

"Did you tell her?" Anthony insisted, pulling across the intersection.

Rae tried to tighten her grip on Anthony's hand, but she was too numb, frozen all the way to her bones.

"I tried," Aiden said.

"What does that mean?" Anthony shot back.

"It means I tried," Aiden answered, a slight edge to his voice. "I explained it all, but I don't know how much she understood. I had to keep her heavily sedated so she wouldn't be able to use her power, so she was only semiconscious. But I told her that the agency killed her mother because her mother was going to expose them for the experiments they'd done on her and the other women in the group. The experiments that gave Rae's mother and Yana's mother their powers."

"That ended up mutating Rae and Yana, too. Don't forget that side effect of the experiments," Anthony reminded him.

"Did she . . . ?" Anthony and Aiden waited while Rae struggled to get the words out of her deadened mouth. "Did she believe you? About my mom?"

There was a long silence from the back of the car. "I don't know," Aiden finally admitted. "I planned to explain everything to her again when I thought it was safe to lower the doses of her drugs. But—"

"But she escaped," Anthony interrupted. "How in the hell did that happen?"

"There was a power surge. It messed up the security system on the doors to her room—the locks opened when they weren't supposed to," Aiden explained. "She got out the back while I was trying to get the system running again."

"She could be in Atlanta already," Rae said. "You are. So she could be." She turned her head, the cold muscles in her neck almost creaking, and stared out at the people on the sidewalk closest to the car. No Yana. Not yet.

"She didn't have any money or—" Aiden began.

"Are you insane?" Anthony burst out. "She doesn't need money. She can inject thoughts into people's heads."

"Let's just figure out how we can find her," Rae said, eyes still searching the sidewalk. "Before she finds me."

"We don't know that she's coming for you," Aiden answered.

She is, though, Rae thought. *I can feel her out there. Coming closer.*

"Where exactly were you keeping her?" Anthony demanded. "How far out of town? We need to retrace her steps."

"I can't tell you that. I can't tell you anything more. I shouldn't even be talking to you now," Aiden said. "If they knew—"

"So you don't care if they kill me?" Rae asked, the novocaine in her veins heating up, turning to acid.

"Of course I care. That's why I'm here. To warn you," Aiden protested. Rae wished she could see his face. She wished she could make him look into her

8

eyes while he pretended to care so much. But he was still crouched on the floor of the backseat.

"And that's it? A warning? That's all you plan to freakin' do?" Anthony exploded. He answered his own question before Aiden could. "There's no way that's happening. You are not getting out of this car until we find Yana."

"Red light," Rae warned Anthony. "Red light!"

Anthony slammed on the brakes. The back door swung open, and Aiden scrambled out into the street. He zigzagged across the lane of oncoming traffic.

"He's gone," Rae said, watching Aiden disappear around a corner.

"Bastard," Anthony muttered. He squeezed Rae's hand so hard, she felt the small bones rub together. "Don't worry," he said. "We don't need him to find Yana."

Maybe we shouldn't be trying to find her, Rae thought. *Maybe it's a mistake, a huge mistake where RaeAnthony ends up dead.*

Yana Savari stopped at the red light. "Red means stop. Green means go," she muttered. Like on the door. Green. So go.

"Do you need help crossing the street?" a voice asked. "You can cross with me."

"Are you . . . me?" Yana replied, turning toward the

voice and peering down at the striped blobby thing that stood next to her. "Are you . . . me?" she repeated when the blobby didn't answer. The words . . . not right. The right ones . . . stuck in the sticky stuff inside her brain.

"I can go get my mommy," the blobby said. Why could Yana understand the blobby words but not make the right words herself? She gave a little growl of frustration, and the blobby backed away. Then the light turned green.

Green, go. Like the door. In the room. Red, red, red, red. Watching, watching. Red, red, red. Then green. Green for go. Like now. Green light. Yana bolted across the street, leaving the blobby behind her. Go, go, go. Something red. Over there. She hesitated, peering at it. No. Not a light. Don't stop. Go, go, go. Run, run, run.

Red. Red light. Means stop. Means door locked. Can't get out. Red light. Yana stopped next to the yellow-and-blue blobby. Not as blobby as the other one. More . . . hard? Solid. More solid. Yana rubbed her eyes. More, more solid. A person. A . . . um . . . what? A . . . a man person. Yellow shirt. Blue jeans.

"Are you okay?" the man asked.

Yana's forehead crinkled as she tried to find the word in her sticky head. She got it, then pushed it out of her mouth. "Yes," she answered.

"You sure?" the man asked.

"Yes." The word came out more easily. Then suddenly there were words everywhere, bouncing around in her head, unstuck. They came spilling out of her mouth. "My mother. My mother. She's dead. Murdered. Someone's got to pay."

Rae's eyelids snapped open. There was someone outside her window. *It's probably just that calico cat,* she told herself as she slipped out of bed. *Or Yana,* she couldn't stop herself from adding.

Cat. Yana. Cat. Yana. The words thudded through her head as she crept up to the window. She pulled the curtain aside an inch and peeked outside.

Mandy Reese smiled at her and gave an apologetic wave. Rae's heart rate returned to normal, and she began to slide the window up, then caught a flash of motion in the darkness. Before she could move, before she could shout a warning, Mandy was thrown to the ground.

By Anthony. 'Cause that's who had come racing across her front lawn. Anthony. He had his knee on Mandy's back, and he was straining to reach . . . a stun gun!

Rae jerked the window all the way up. "Anthony, no!" she cried. "It's Mandy. It's *Mandy.*"

Instantly Anthony jerked his knee off Mandy's

back. He stood up and gently helped her to her feet. "Are you okay?" he asked. "I thought you were Yana."

"Yana?" Mandy exclaimed, fear giving her voice a jagged edge. "Why would Yana—"

"You guys have to be quiet. We don't want to wake up my dad," Rae cautioned them. "Go to the front door. I'll let you in." Without waiting for an answer, Rae quickly threw on the jeans and shirt she'd been wearing today, then hurried out of her bedroom and down the stairs. She turned the lock on the front door slowly, but it still made a click that sounded as loud as a gunshot to Rae's ears. She hesitated a moment, listening. But she didn't hear any movement from her dad's room, so she swung open the door, gestured Anthony and Mandy inside, and led them back into her room.

"Are you okay?" she asked Mandy as soon as she'd shut the door behind them.

"Yeah. I'm fine," she said, speaking half to Rae and half to Anthony. "But what's the deal with Yana? I thought Aiden had her locked away, loaded with drugs."

"She escaped," Anthony answered.

"God. Oh God." Mandy sat down on the edge of Rae's bed.

"You're safe," Anthony told her. "Yana's got no reason to be coming after you. She probably didn't even see you that night in the cabin, and there's no way she knows that you used your power to help track her down."

"I'm not worried about that," Mandy said. She turned to Rae. "But I should be asking if you're okay, not the other way around. What she tried to do to you at the cabin—" Mandy shook her head as if she couldn't stand to even think about it.

"I'm okay, really," Rae told her. It was a lie, but she wanted to keep Mandy out of this. Mandy'd done enough for Rae already. Her mother was in the same group that Rae's mother and Yana's mother were in. And Mandy's genes had been screwed up by the experiments that had been done on her mom, just the way Rae's and Yana's had been screwed up.

But Mandy didn't know that until Yana took Rae hostage. Then Aiden and Anthony had told Mandy the truth about herself. They'd told Mandy that she had some kind of psychic ability that would start showing itself when she was at the height of puberty. They said that they thought her power—whatever it was—might help them save Rae. So Mandy, even though she barely knew Rae, had agreed to let Aiden give her an injection of hormones to bring out her power right away. And it was some power, too—it turned out that Mandy could touch an item of clothing belonging to someone and "see" that person. Actually, more like *be* the person for a few minutes. She'd used

Rae's sweater to figure out where Yana'd taken Rae.

"Why don't I believe you?" Mandy asked Rae.

"Because you're a smart girl," Anthony muttered.

"Why were you even over here tonight?" Rae asked, not wanting to drag Mandy deeper into Rae's personal nightmare. The girl was only fourteen. She should be out doing . . . fun stuff. Normal stuff.

Mandy started making a little braid in her long, light brown hair. "It's stupid. I'm sorry. I shouldn't have come running over here so late."

"Bathroom," Anthony mouthed at Rae, then quietly left her and Mandy alone.

"It's not stupid," Rae said as she sat down next to Mandy. "When I found out I could get thoughts from fingerprints, I completely freaked. Are you freaking about your powers?"

"Yeah," Mandy admitted. "Plus that hormone shot did something to my breasts. I wanted them to be bigger, but they've been growing so fast, they ache."

Rae winced. "Ouch. Mandy, you know how sorry—"

"Oh, shut up," Mandy interrupted. "I told you I don't want you to apologize. Anyway, that's not why I came over."

Rae picked up one of the dark green pillows off the head of her bed and cradled it to her chest. "So what is going on?"

Anthony came back in and hesitated. He raised an eyebrow at Rae. "Is it okay if Anthony's here?" she asked Mandy.

"Sure. But like I said, it's nothing that I needed to talk to you about in the middle of the night. Not with the Yana thing happening," Mandy said.

"We both owe you," Anthony told her as he sat down in Rae's black leather desk chair. "If you have a problem, we want to help."

Do I have a great guy or what? Rae thought before she turned her full attention back to Mandy.

"My sister, Emma? She's always been sickeningly good. She always does her homework right away. She tutors these kids at the elementary school. God, she irons her jeans," Mandy said. "At least that's how she used to be. But since my mom died . . . was murdered," Mandy corrected herself. She paused, her eyes glazing over. "I can still hardly believe that crazy scientist guy killed her," she murmured.

Rae knew exactly how Mandy felt. Steve Mercer, the man who'd shocked and drugged and radiated her mother—and Yana's and Mandy's—had murdered Rae's mother, too. He'd gone crazy and killed the members of the group he thought were dangerous to society. He would have killed Rae if the agency that funded the experiments—the agency where Aiden used to work—hadn't killed him first. It was so eerie knowing that somebody had actually gone after her mother like that, and she could only imagine how much scarier it would be for Mandy, since she'd already been a teenager when it happened. Rae had only been a baby when her mother died.

"So your sister," Anthony prodded gently.

Mandy gave her head a little shake. "Right," she said. "I touched this shirt of hers, and I *was* her, you know?" Rae and Anthony nodded. "And I . . . she was making out with this gross guy Zeke. She never would have even spoken to scum like him when Mom was alive. And I could tell . . . I could *feel* how into him she is. He's going to hurt her. I know it. But there's no way she's going to listen to her stupid baby sister about something like that."

"Maybe he's not as bad as he seems," Anthony said, using his feet to turn the chair back and forth and back and forth. "What makes you think he's scum?" He gave an extra-hard shove with his feet and spun the chair completely around.

"How about the fact that he's stoned pretty much every second of the day?" Mandy answered. "I think he might even be dealing a little. What if Emma starts doing that crap, too? She practically has this scholarship to UCLA in the bag, but she's going to totally screw it up if she keeps hanging with Zeke."

Mandy started wrapping her little braid around

her finger. Rae'd seen her do that before when she was stressed. God, she practically pulled the hair out of her head.

"Look, tomorrow's Saturday. How about if I help you check out this Zeke guy?" Rae said. She gently pulled the little braid out of Mandy's fingers.

"Don't you think we should be—" Anthony began.

Rae shook her head. "I think we should just do what we'd usually do, 'cause what other choice do we have?" She smiled at Mandy. "And what I'd usually be doing is trying to get a scum reading on your sister's guy."

"Thanks," Mandy said. "I . . . just thanks." She turned back to Anthony. "But you were going to say something about looking for Yana, right?"

Anthony glanced at Rae, then slowly nodded.

"You're right," Mandy told him. "We have to help my sister, but we have to find Yana first. So what do we do?"

Rae tilted her head to the side. Mandy sounded so much like Rae and Anthony's friend Jesse. Eager to help, ready to throw herself into something extremely dangerous for Rae's sake. In the middle of all the horrible stuff that had happened to Rae recently, she'd made some pretty amazing friends.

Anthony coughed. "That's basically the problem," he said. "We don't know what to do. We have

17

no idea where Yana could be right now." He shrugged. "So we just have to wait," he said, his voice tightening on the last word.

Mandy narrowed her eyes in concentration. "Maybe not," she said. "Maybe there *is* something we can do. Well, something *I* can do."

Rae frowned. "Mandy, I don't want you—"

"No, she's right," Anthony said, his eyes taking on an excited gleam. "And don't worry, Rae, she won't be in any danger."

What was Rae missing here? She stared at both of them, then finally got it.

"Your power," she blurted.

"Yes," Mandy said. "Anthony, can you get me something of Yana's? Something she's worn?"

"Definitely," Anthony answered. "I'll bring it to you tomorrow. And once we know where Yana is, we go after her."

God, Rae thought, shivering. *Am I going to end up bringing them both into something none of us will survive?*